"You think I'm here to *blackmail* you?"

Joshua gazed coolly into her blazing eyes. "You found out who I was—who I'm engaged to—and figured that you were in a perfect position to threaten or disrupt my wedding plans."

That was the height of irony, considering what she had come here to do. "I'm sorry to disappoint you, but I had no idea who you were until a few minutes ago," Regan gritted. "And it makes not one iota of difference to me. I have no interest in you."

To her fury he grinned. "You were interested in me every which way that night in the apartment...."

"I treat all my one-night stands like that!"

SUSAN NAPIER

The Revenge Affair

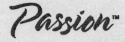

Passion™

HARLEQUIN®

TORONTO • NEW YORK • LONDON
AMSTERDAM • PARIS • SYDNEY • HAMBURG
STOCKHOLM • ATHENS • TOKYO • MILAN • MADRID
PRAGUE • WARSAW • BUDAPEST • AUCKLAND

For
Barbara and Peter Clendon,
Carol and Helen
for their friendship and energy,
encouraging me to write
and others to read

ISBN 0-373-12062-1

THE REVENGE AFFAIR

First North American Publication 1999.

Visit us at www.romance.net

Printed in U.S.A.

CHAPTER ONE

As THE lift doors opened Regan smoothed her sweaty palms down the side-seams of her classic black sheath and took a deep breath, beating back the niggle of doubt which had invaded her rebellious confidence during the swooping upward journey.

She had come this far—she couldn't chicken out now!

She stepped jerkily out of the padded lift into the stark luxury of a marble foyer, her slim body taut with tension. The rarefied air was unnaturally still and quiet, as if the ragged end of the evening rush-hour funnelling through Auckland's inner-city streets far below didn't exist.

Regan looked around, her straight black brows arching in faint disapproval. There was nothing warm or welcoming about the formal entranceway to the three apartments sharing the fourteenth floor. The lush tropical foliage growing out of huge glazed pots only partially offset the chilly atmosphere of intimidating elegance. The glossy, impervious surfaces and pale biscuit-coloured matt paint on the upper walls created a neutral environment which bordered on the boring. The only jarring note was the glaring red eye of a state-of-the-art security camera placed high up against the ceiling.

The lift doors hissed shut behind Regan's back with unexpected swiftness, the discreet thunk and faint whine of the descending mechanism making her nerves jump as she realised that she was temporarily cut off from her quickest avenue of escape.

It seemed somehow symbolic, as if Fate was making the choice for her—urging her to proceed with her audacious plans for the evening, chiding her for her cowardly hesitation.

Regan's fingers bunched into unconscious fists, her plum-dark nails digging into her clammy palms as she studied the gold numbering etched into the marble wall opposite the lift.

A discreet arrow directed her to the left, where a short corridor framed a dark wooden door recessed deep into the pale wall.

As she moved towards her destination she was uncomfortably aware of the video camera on the wall behind her. The notion that some faceless security man might be watching her even now, and speculating on the reasons for her visit, made her want to break into a guilty dash, but she forced herself to maintain a graceful stroll as she moved out of sight around the corner.

It had never occurred to her that her presence might be recorded on video. She had naively imagined that, for the protection of both sides in this arrangement, everything would remain conveniently off the record.

In the unnatural hush the delicate, gold-chased heels of her black evening sandals sounded out tiny exclamation marks against the veined marble floor, punctuating her nervous progress.

Just think of it as a date, Regan repeated to herself, trying to emulate the brash attitude displayed by her nineteen-year-old flatmate and her trendy clique of friends. Unfortunately the thought wasn't very liberating for a woman who hadn't had a casual date in over five years!

Oh, it was all very well for Lisa and her cynical cousin Cleo, whose modelling careers had taught them to regard males as interchangeable accessories, but such casual insouciance was alien to Regan's experience of men. In the five months since she had answered the ad to share a flat with the scatterbrained Lisa and cheerfully laid-back

Saleena she had come to realise how sheltered she had been in her previous existence. She had always naively believed that mutual respect and shared interests were the essence of any relationship between a man and a woman. Her strict upbringing had precluded the startling idea that one might choose a man purely according to one's mood, rather than because he appeared to be a sound, long-term emotional investment.

Tonight promised to be a revelation in more ways than one!

Regan moistened her dry lips. Oh, she had plenty of confidence in her social skills when it came to playing hostess, or circulating amongst groups of friends or business acquaintances, but she knew little of the modern protocols governing the intimate entertaining of a man one-on-one, so to speak.

One-on-one...

A shiver of delicious apprehension sizzled down her spine at the wanton image that sprang immediately to mind. Her pale skin warmed to a delicate blush as she pictured the searingly intimate circumstances in which this evening would probably end.

Of course, that was only if she *wanted* the evening to end that way, she reassured herself. It was purely ladies' choice—or so she had been told—but she wasn't so naive as to believe that the man she had come here to meet wouldn't have intimate expectations of his own.

Erotic expectations that *she* was supposed to fulfil to the max...

Regan's courage hit another serious speed wobble. Oh, God, she must have been mad to think that she could carry this off! She was an utter fraud. How did a woman who couldn't even inspire passion in the man she loved expect to be believable in the role of sexy, sultry playmate to a total stranger?

The moral teachings of a lifetime rose up to haunt her. This was the first step down the slippery slope to complete depravity. To what depths had she sunk to even consider such wickedness? Wasn't she disgusted with herself for betraying her cherished ideals?

No! A hot thrust of bitter remembrance stiffened her wavering resolve. She tossed her midnight-dark head in a gesture of angry defiance, fanning the blunt ends of her silky-straight bob across creamy shoulders laid bare by her sleeveless dress. Below the scooped neckline the snug black fabric tightened across her small breasts as she sucked in another steadying breath, struggling to control the acid rage which had been brewing and bubbling inside her for weeks, blistering her with shame, and self-contempt for her own weakness.

No! Regan's violet eyes glittered with repressed pain and fury. She had nothing to be ashamed of…she was betraying nothing that hadn't already been proved utterly unworthy of her faith.

She was no longer a pathetic, self-deluded, gullible fool, hiding her head in the sand to avoid having to confront the crude realities of life.

And the reality was that up until now it had been *Regan* who was morally out of step with the modern world.

Plenty of women her age—ordinary, *normal*, well-adjusted twenty-five-year-old women—wouldn't see anything wrong with what she was going to do. Regan was unattached, independent and answerable only to herself. No one was going to be hurt by her actions tonight. It was about time she adopted an outlook more in tune with the rest of her generation—more open-minded and willing to experiment with what life had to offer.

To catch up with the sexual revolution!

Tonight she was going to prove that Regan Frances was a sophisticated, passionate, desirable woman—a sexual be-

ing who could treat the giving and taking of pleasure with
the same casualness that men seemed to enjoy. Then, and
only then, would she feel truly liberated from the travesty
of her marriage, and the crushing humiliations of the past
few weeks.

She came to a halt before the deep-set door, breathlessly
aware that the definitive moment had arrived.

Just treat it as a date.

Reaching out to press the doorbell, Regan was dismayed
to see the fine tremor in her hand that twice made her finger
miss its target. In the shiny brass surround she saw a dis-
torted view of her own face, all mouth and eyes. She licked
her dry lips, adding extra gloss to the dark plum colour
which Lisa proclaimed was the ultimate in sultry glamour,
and steeled herself to take another stab at the button.

As she did so the thin white strip on the ring-finger of
her left hand mocked her timidity, and another hot jolt of
temper kicked the normally tender bow of her mouth into
a vengeful curve.

Wouldn't Michael be astonished to see his boring little
sexless doormat of a wife *now*! she thought viciously, giving the silent bell a second defiant jab.

Except, of course, he couldn't—because to her certain
knowledge Michael Frances wasn't gazing benevolently
down from a blissful heaven of the soul; he was too busy
burning in fiery hell!

On that deeply gratifying thought the door opened…and
Regan's heart dropped like a stone into her sexy shoes.

CHAPTER TWO

INSTEAD of the virile, attractive, sexy sophisticate Regan had been praying for, a skinny, swarthy, wrinkled old man as bald as a billiard ball stood in the doorway.

Even though she was only five-foot-three, Regan towered over him in her slender heels, and not even his faultlessly cut black suit could disguise a shrunken frame and unmistakably bandy legs. As if to compensate for his shiny pate his salt-and-pepper eyebrows were luxuriantly bushy, springing upwards in fanning tufts which give him a permanently surprised expression.

He had to be sixty if he was a day!

Thunderstruck, Regan's first impulse was to bolt, but she mastered the knee-jerk impulse and swallowed hard as the wizened gnome dipped his head to one side.

'Bonsoir, mam'selle.'

A horrified giggle swelled in her throat. Was he really French, or did he think a suave foreign accent would make him more attractive to women?

Oh, God, it had never occurred to her that she might have to vamp a rich old fogey! On the contrary, Cleo had boasted that all the 'social liaisons' arranged by her ambitious ex-boyfriend were with perfectly agreeable single men who were simply too busy making gobs of money to sustain ongoing relationships with women. They preferred the no-maintenance alternative provided by Derek's informal network of 'friends'—attractive, sophisticated, obliging women, who could be relied upon to accept an invitation to a good night out without pouting about short notice and who cheerfully vanished when their attentions were no longer required to boost the male ego—or libido…

Knowing Cleo's elastic standards, Regan should have realised that her idea of 'perfectly agreeable' covered an awful lot of ground. 'Seriously rich' was probably her main criteria of judgement.

The old man was still patiently awaiting a response to his greeting, and the puzzled enquiry in the shrewd blue eyes caused a faint flicker of hope in her breast. But a quick sideways glance at the number by the bell told Regan that she hadn't made a mistake.

'Uh—good evening,' she ventured, pinning on a smile that quivered with effort around the edges as she realised that she didn't even know his *name*!

To give herself time to think she ducked her head to fumble in her beaded evening bag for the card which had been thrust into her hand a scant hour earlier.

'I know I'm a little late, but—uh—Derek sent me,' she blurted, holding out the business card with the apartment's address scribbled on the back.

A gnarled hand accepted the card, the startling eyebrows rumpling like woolly caterpillars as he frowningly studied it, then her.

'But you are not who is expected,' he said suspiciously, still standing squarely in the doorway, barring her entrance. His gaze roamed down over the shimmery black stockings encasing her slender calves, and back up to the hemline modestly skimming her knees and the regrettably slight cleavage exposed by the low-cut bodice. He shook his head, his thin lips pursed in what she instantly interpreted as disappointment. 'You are *not* Mam'selle Cleo…'

Perversely, Regan was outraged by his rejection. Instead of gratefully seizing on the excuse to withdraw with her dignity still intact, she lifted her chin, her small, triangular face paling with anger, her wide-set violet eyes darkening to the colour of fresh bruises as she prepared to do battle for her wounded pride.

Adrenaline pumped through her veins, fresh fuel to the smouldering anger inside her. How dared he dismiss her with such effortless ease?

This time she was not going to meekly bow to male judgement of her feminine worth. Since Michael had died she had learned that he had cheated her out of a lot more than just money. No man was going to get away with making her feel like a failure—not ever again!

It suddenly became vital that she wrap this contemptible little weasel around her little finger.

So she wasn't what he had expected—she wasn't a tall, willowy, full-breasted redhead, with emerald eyes and legs that went on for ever. That didn't mean she was any less of a woman!

'Cleo couldn't make it,' she told him coolly. 'She's indisposed.'

That was putting it delicately! Not half an hour ago Lisa's beauteous cousin had been sprawled on her hands and knees on a cold bathroom floor, her flawless complexion a putrid shade of green, her glamorous red hair dangling over the white china toilet bowl as she alternately retched and moaned, vile curses spewing from her pale lips as she vowed never to mix curry and cocktails again.

'And so...this means Monsieur Derek asks for you to come in her place?'

Regan sucked in her cheeks, trying for that haughty, bored model look that she had seen Lisa practising endlessly in the mirror.

'It was very much a last-minute kind of a thing—Cleo got sick and I was available,' she said, adroitly avoiding an outright lie.

She hoped that he wasn't going to suggest checking her story with Derek. But why should he bother? As Cleo had pointed out, there was nothing illegal involved, no need for fear on either side. Derek Clarke's discreet little sideline, designed to ingratiate himself with potentially useful colleagues and clients, was successful precisely because it was so casual.

'I see,' he said slowly, relaxing his stance. 'And you are...?'

'Ev—' She bit her lip. She had already decided that Regan was too distinctive a name, too easy to trace. She *had* intended to shelter behind her middle name, but now it occurred to her that Evangeline was just as singular as Regan. 'I— It's Eve,' she corrected hurriedly. 'My name is Eve.'

'Mam'selle...Eve.' His deliberate hesitation and wry intonation suggested he knew she was lying, and she flushed with guilt.

'I am Pierre.' He smiled suddenly—a splitting grin which rendered him uglier than ever. He turned sideways, inviting her inside with a broad, sweeping gesture of his arm.

'Unfortunately, Monsieur is running rather late this evening,' he said, his accent rolling off his tongue in an unmistakably genuine purr. 'He has rung to say that he is held up in a business meeting and asked me to deliver his apologies. He says that he will be home as soon as possible. Fortunately, he informs me, the dinner you are to attend does not begin until a fashionably late hour. In the meantime he suggests that you relax and enjoy a drink, and make free of the apartment while you are waiting. Monsieur has an excellent home entertainment centre...'

'Monsieur?' Regan repeated faintly, the blood pounding in her ears as she realised how close she had come to making a fresh idiot of herself.

The blind date that she had hijacked from Cleo wasn't with a wizened old gnome old enough to be her grandfather!

Pierre wasn't the man she was supposed to flirt with, flatter and seduce.

Regan's hopes soared as the evening ahead regained its tantalising promise...the wicked allure of pleasures previously denied her by her husband's secret indifference—the perfect revenge for years of his perfunctory lovemaking!

Her smile of euphoric relief was so dazzlingly different from the strained rictus that Regan had worn since the door opened that Pierre blinked.

'You're the *butler,*' she guessed happily as she floated past his bandy figure into the apartment, mentally scolding herself for jumping to hasty conclusions. If he couldn't even spare the time to pick up his own women, a wealthy workaholic businessman would scarcely be likely to be answering doors!

'I don't believe I have a title, as such,' said Pierre. 'I merely assist Monsieur with his domestic arrangements.'

The self-effacing comment was belied by the ring of pride in his voice as he preceded her down a short flight of stairs which wrapped around the curving wall of glass bricks screening the entranceway from the main body of the apartment.

'I bet you do the lion's share,' Regan murmured drily, her heels sinking into thick white carpet that she imagined would require meticulous care.

'*Mais, non.* Monsieur does not own such a pet,' Pierre said blandly. 'Except when the survival of the species is at stake, he does not approve of wild beasts being held in captivity...'

Regan swallowed a grin. 'Is that why he's not married?' she shot back, her flippancy cloaking her urgent need to assure herself that the little information she *did* have was at least correct on that one, all-important point.

Pierre's eyebrows twitched in acknowledgment of her riposte. 'Monsieur is the most intelligent and civilised of men,' he observed primly as he reached the bottom of the stairs and turned to watch her join him, 'although a certain degree of wildness is only to be expected of healthy males in their prime.' The fugitive gleam of mischief in the old eyes glowed even brighter. 'He certainly does not yet regard himself as being on the endangered species list...'

So... Unmarried. Healthy. Intelligent. Prime...with a dash of wildness thrown in for good measure. Regan lowered her lashes to hide her surge of terrified elation.

No wonder Cleo had been so furious about having to cry off!

She had come hammering on the door of the flat a scant hour earlier, stridently upset when she'd discovered that her cousin wasn't home and Regan had no idea of her whereabouts.

'There was a message on the answer-machine when I got back from work to say that she was going out to some party and wouldn't be here for dinner,' Regan had said, still annoyed that Lisa had conveniently forgotten that it was her turn to cook.

'But she can't be out! I was sure she'd be here—I need Lisa *now*!' Cleo wailed. 'It's a matter of life and death!' She barged inside with none of her usual grace. 'What about Saleena?' she demanded raggedly. 'Is *she* here?'

Regan fell back, shaking her head. 'Evening aerobics classes.' Saleena worked part-time at the local gym to supplement her student loan while she studied for a degree in Sport and Recreation. Like Lisa, she was extremely pretty and always game for a laugh, although—being two years older and a great deal more intelligent—her behaviour and attitudes were thankfully more mature.

Cleo screamed, a low, heart-felt shriek of frustration.

'Can I help?' Regan sighed, too accustomed to Cleo's histrionics to be truly concerned. Perhaps she had run out of nail polish for her synthetic talons. Dressed to the glittering hilt, and made up to model-girl perfection, she was obviously on her way somewhere trendy and expensive.

'You!' Cleo uttered an insulting laugh that ended in a muffled choke as her exquisite face turned suddenly from honey-gold tan to swamp-green and she dashed towards the bathroom, clutching her concave belly.

When she tottered out and collapsed on the couch in the lounge without bothering to artistically drape her limbs for the best visual effect, Regan knew that she was genuinely at the end of her tether.

It turned out that what Cleo had convinced herself was merely a lingering all-day hangover had developed into something debilitatingly nasty at both ends, and she was frantic to find a substitute for some hot date that an ex-boyfriend, Derek, had fixed her up with for that night.

'I've been trying to call Derek to tell him I didn't think I could make it, but he's not answering his stupid phone,' Cleo shrilled, 'and I haven't been able to find anyone to fill in for me, not this late on a Friday night…

'I thought I might manage it if I took a few pills, and they seemed to work for a while, but now I feel even worse,' Cleo groaned. 'In the taxi I thought I was going to throw up, so I told the driver to drop me off here—I knew Lisa would help…' She looked up at Regan through a tangle of red hair, her green eyes tearful with angry self-pity. 'I'm supposed to be there in half an hour and I *can't* simply not turn up, because I was supposed to escort this guy out to some fancy dinner— Oh, God!'

The mere suggestion of food prompted another mad scramble to reach the bathroom on time.

When she finally emerged on wobbly legs Regan offered to call a doctor, but Cleo was adamant that she didn't need one. 'I just want to lie down for a while,' she said shakily, homing in on Lisa's cluttered bedroom and crashing gratefully across the unmade bed. 'I have to warn Derek,' she moaned piteously. 'His phone number's on his card in my evening bag—I think I dropped it in the lounge—keep trying him for me, will you? And if you get through, tell him what's happened.'

'Why don't you just phone your date yourself and tell him you're ill?' Regan asked, unable to understand her obsession. What did one broken date matter to a woman who hardly ever went out with the same man twice?

'Because I don't have his phone number, that's why—only Derek's card, with the address I'm supposed to go written on the back and the time I'm supposed to be there!' Cleo croaked, rolling over onto her back. 'Hell, Derek'll *kill* me if I mess this one up for him—he said he could get some really good accounts from this guy.' Her former boyfriend was in advertising, and staying on friendly terms with him had landed Cleo several plum modelling assignments. 'But what in the hell am I supposed to do, for God's sake?' she said, panic turning to petulance. 'It's not my fault I got sick!'

She dragged her arm from across her bloodshot eyes and glared belligerently at Regan, who wisely held her tongue. In her opinion Cleo's hectic, party-loving lifestyle involved too much alcohol and too little food, and Lisa's puppyish admiration for her glamorous elder cousin was leading her down the same path.

Her silence appeared to mollify Cleo, who interpreted it as sympathetic agreement, and in between violent bouts with the re-emerging curry she allowed the rest of the story to emerge: how Derek regularly set up dates for Cleo and some of her girlfriends with wealthy single men, the kind of men who were happy to reward a pretty woman who escorted them around town with expensive trinkets if she was willing to round off the evening in bed.

'You mean Derek is a *pimp!*' Regan gasped, her eyes

rounding as Cleo's busy social life suddenly acquired a shocking new perspective.

'Of course he's not!' Cleo roused from her torpor to snap. 'He just does a few favours for people who might one day be in a position to do *him* a business favour in return, that's all. None of us makes any *money* out of it; it's not like it's a call-girl operation, for God's sake—so you can stop looking so bug-eyed with disapproval! It's just consenting adults being introduced to each together and…well, consenting!'

After her initial mental recoil Regan was filled with a morbid fascination. 'But…you said that the men rewarded you for sleeping with them…' she probed.

'Yes, but only with jewellery, not *money*,' Cleo tossed back scornfully, as if it made all the difference in the world. And perhaps it wasn't just semantics, thought Regan, her emotions churning in dark turmoil. At least both participants in the transaction knew the score, and there was no intention to deceive with any romantic pretence of love and caring.

What would it be like to make love with someone on a purely physical basis? she wondered with a shivery thrill. Without the pretences. With a stranger. Someone who had no preconceived notions about your desirability, or your ability to respond, who just wanted a lusty romp in the hay with no questions asked…

An idea, as bizarre and impractical as it was wicked and daring, slyly insinuated itself into her consciousness. After all that had happened was she going to continue to allow herself to be a victim, crippled by the lies with which Michael had ruthlessly manipulated their marriage, or was she prepared to reach out and grab at a chance to shatter his power over her for ever?

'A glamorous party, some recreational sex and a gold bracelet or a pair of diamond studs to wear home afterwards...what more could a girl ask of a date?' Cleo boasted feebly, waving a limp hand and drawing Regan's attention to the thick chased-gold bangle clasped around her bony wrist.

She stared at it as if hypnotised, goaded to ask, 'But how can you? I mean, what would happen if you found the man—you know...physically repulsive?'

'I don't *have* to have sex with them if I don't want to, it's not *compulsory*,' Cleo said through gritted teeth, distracted by another threatening liquid rumble in her belly. 'Derek never promises a guaranteed score—that would be tacky. Anyway, sometimes all *they* want is to show up somewhere with a flirtatious woman dangling off their arm. But most times it doesn't end up platonic, because I don't see anything wrong with sleeping with a guy you've just met if he turns you on, and since Derek only does favours for the movers and the shakers of this world...well, power's a great aphrodisiac in itself, isn't it?

'It so happens most of them are a hell of lot more virile and attractive than the average Joe Loser who tries to pick you up in a bar and thinks the price of a drink entitles him to a night in the sack! As if!'

Regan had been an earnest, nineteen-year-old virgin studying pre-law at university when she had first met Michael. She had never been picked up in a bar either before or since. She had never even wondered what it might be like.

Until now.

Now she was wondering about all sorts of things that she had never before considered.

'What's his name?' she ventured. 'The man you're supposed to meet tonight?'

'Oh, God, who *cares*?' Cleo groaned, rolling off the bed to hit the floor running. 'Look, just get hold of Derek and let him sort things out, OK? I don't give a stuff what happens—all I want is to be left alone to spew my guts out in peace!'

So Regan left her wallowing in her misery and went to rifle the contents of the sequinned purse she picked up from the floor of the lounge. From it she extracted Derek's business card, and, after a moment of shocked contemplation, one of the packets of condoms that Cleo obviously considered essential dating equipment. Surely she hadn't expected to use all four packets in *one night*!

Pushing that daunting thought aside, and acutely conscious of time ticking away, Regan hurried through her nervous preparations, hampered by her restricted access to the bathroom. Luckily she had washed her hair that morning before work, so a quick shower sufficed, and she borrowed some of Lisa's manufacturers' samples to experiment with a bolder style of make-up which made her violet eyes look provocatively large and heavy-lidded. Her hand shook as she carefully applied a thick coating of black mascara, her mother's oft-repeated catch-phrase ringing silently in her ears: *A painted woman is the devil's handmaiden.*

Fortunately for her nagging conscience, Saleena arrived home just as Regan was ready to leave, and she was able to gratefully hand over the responsibility for their miserable guest.

'I was going to study for next week's exam,' Saleena had protested mildly, her exotic brown eyes taking in Regan's uncharacteristic glamour. 'But I suppose I can keep an eye on Miss Chunderful while I'm at it, to make sure she doesn't drown in the toilet. Where're you off to?'

'I have a date,' Regan replied, fussing with her hair in the hall mirror so that she didn't have to look her flatmate in the face.

'No kidding? Cool!' Saleena approved the unprecedented event with her customary laid-back nonchalance. 'Who with?'

'Oh, no one you'd know,' said Regan vaguely, not about to confess that she didn't know either. For all her fun-loving personality, Saleena had a tendency to be a little over-protective where Regan was concerned, perceptive enough to realise what a culture shock it had been for her to move from a ritzy house in the suburbs to a cramped inner-city flat with two gregarious bachelorettes.

'OK. Have a good time.' No one could claim that Saleena Patel couldn't take a subtle hint to mind her own business. She flashed a cheerful smile. 'Did Lisa at least do the food shopping for tonight, do you know?'

'No, but after I listened to her message I went and got a few things down the road.' Regan was halfway out of the door before she recognised a serious flaw in her plan. She hurried back to find Saleena in the kitchen, unpacking the small plastic shopping bag that Regan had left on the bench-top.

'By the way, if Cleo asks, tell her not to worry—everything's sorted out as far as Derek's concerned and she can forget all about it, because the whole thing was apparently all off anyway…'

'What thing?' Saleena asked, opening a packet of dry pasta, and when Regan's face pinkened betrayingly she grinned and rolled her eyes. 'Oh, one of Derek's high-flying pals was supposed to be in town looking for some action, huh? No wonder Cleo's yowling so loud in there—she thinks she's missing out on her next jewellery fix!'

'You *know* about that?'

'Sure,' Saleena admitted casually, snacking on a brittle strand of spaghetti. 'She even tried to get me interested in joining Derek's swinging circle at one stage, but I told her I'd rather choose my own partners, thanks…'

Saleena was so blasé in her acceptance that Regan was once more made aware of her embarrassing naivety. What had been a shock to her was already common knowledge to her flatmates, and probably most of their friends. None of them was married, and all of them seemed to be sexually active, so doubtless they didn't see anything so shocking in Cleo's behaviour.

Regan contrived to act blasé now, as Pierre ushered her further into the huge, fan-shaped living space dominated by a wraparound view of the city skyline. Soft up-lights on the smooth walls and on slender free-standing lamp-bases revealed a room that was a symphony of delicate colour—subtle, warm hues blended and contrasted to present an impression of exquisite harmony. Outside the full-length windows, the wide, sweeping curve of a marble ledge echoed the various curves within—the round support pillars, the round marble coffee table centred between two long, half-round couches in blush-coloured leather and the semi-circular padded chairs dotted about the room, facing the fanned-out city. Away to one end, a few more steps led up to a raised dining area with a huge oval wooden table, and beyond that, presumably, to the kitchen. At the other end of the room was a curving corridor whose even subtler lighting suggested...the bedrooms?

Regan hastily turned her head, forcing herself to concentrate on the main room.

'It's beautiful!' she murmured, and then was annoyed with herself for sounding awed. A sophisticated woman of the world would take such beauty for granted. Knowing Cleo, the first thing she would have done was demand an ashtray! 'Monsieur has impeccable taste,' she added, with a suggestion of dry mockery.

'*Merci.*' Pierre shifted his bandy legs, clicking his polished black heels and inclining his head. 'This is a corporate apartment, used by many executives, so it must fulfil many functions. It was I who hired the interior designer and advised on and approved her designs, as well as supervising the physical decorating work.'

'You!' This time her jaw did drop at the idea of this ugly little man helping create such beauty.

'Appearances can be deceptive,' he replied modestly, un-offended.

Tell me about it! thought Regan evilly, her hand spasming on her purse as another spurt of anger shot through her veins. Michael had been blessed with sunny good looks—blond hair, boyish features, guileless blue eyes, and a white smile that predicated a charmingly frank and open manner.

Who would have believed that behind that golden façade had been a lying tongue and a cheating black heart—a man without honour? Not Regan. Right up to the night that Michael had wrapped his precious BMW status symbol around a tree she had believed that they had a secure and happy marriage, with only minor problems to cloud their shared contentment. She had admired her husband's dedication to work and respected his ambition to succeed. Only after he had died and the huge, unexpected bills had started to roll in had she begun to re-examine her former contentment, and come to realise that her willingness to overlook the flaws in their relationship had played right into Michael's cheating hands.

Over the following months, as the mess his lies had created had grown to staggering proportions, she had gradually been forced to the painful conclusion that, to all intents and purposes, she had been sleeping with a stranger for the four years of their marriage!

So what she was going to do tonight was not so very different after all, she thought bitterly, as she watched Pierre begin to put his personal orders into action.

He moved across to open the curved doors of a teak cabinet, revealing a wide-screen television and the most complex stereo system that Regan had ever seen. Concealed in a false support pillar next to the cabinet were racks of video tapes and CDs, arranged with alphabetical precision.

Pierre settled her on one of the demi-couches with the re-mote controls and furnished her with a vodka and tonic with a twist of lime in a chilled crystal glass, setting it down on a round side-table on top of a deftly folded cocktail napkin. He told her that the bathroom was down the curving corridor to her right and if she had a question, or required a refill for her drink, she could summon Pierre merely by pressing one of the hidden buttons strategically placed around the room, or she could help herself from the super-latively stocked bar which opened out from yet another mock-pillar.

Left alone, Regan drank her vodka quickly, in the hope that it might help her to relax. Except for warming the pit of her belly it didn't seem to have any appreciable effect, so she guiltily fixed herself another, embarrassed at the idea of summoning Pierre back so soon...he might think he had a rampant alcoholic on his hands!

Sipping more slowly, she ignored the television and chose a CD of smoky ballads from the wonderfully eclectic selection of music, and after a bit of clumsy experimenta-tion managed to get the remote control to set the volume and balance at the perfect level for her position in the room. As she lounged back on the feather-soft couch in her splen-did isolation she reflected that she could get used to being ultra-rich!

The most difficult part about flatting was the lack of pri-vacy. As an only child Regan had been closely monitored by her over-strict mother, but Michael had worked such long hours—or at least, he had *said* that he was working— that during her marriage she had got used to the quiet free-dom of having the whole house to herself for hours on end. In the flat there seemed to be a constant flow of visitors and phone calls and emotional upheavals, accompanied by the loud, head-banging music that Lisa adored.

However, all the activity *did* serve as a welcome distraction from her own weighty problems, Regan acknowledged. And although Lisa and Saleena outstripped her in street-smarts, Regan was the one they turned to when they wanted down-to-earth advice on practical matters—like how to get a pizza stain out of a silk camisole or how to fill in their tax returns. Because she had studied law, she was a valuable source of information for friends who had disputes with their landlords or whose sleazy boyfriends had stashed a joint in their handbags. It didn't matter to them that Regan had dropped out of her degree the previous semester, a year before she was due to graduate, it only mattered that her informed opinion was free. To Regan what mattered was that she felt *valued*, something that her shredded confidence had badly needed.

Pierre drifted back with more murmured apologies for the elusive Monsieur and offered her a small plate of delectable canapés and a glass of champagne. Thinking that it would be unwise to mix her drinks, Regan declined the latter and hungrily consumed the former.

Her stomach gurgled in gratitude. Lunch had been a hurried sandwich at her desk and breakfast had been a mere kick-start from a cup of espresso. In the last few weeks her normally healthy appetite had dwindled to almost nothing, but now she found herself suddenly utterly ravenous.

She pressed the button concealed under a side-table, and when Pierre appeared with startling speed and stealth she sheepishly asked if there were any more canapés.

'They really were delicious,' she added, to excuse her greed. 'You must have a splendid cook.'

'But that is me.' After a couple of vodkas, his ugliness of grin seemed actually endearing. 'I am, after all, a Frenchman, and we excel at such things. I am pleased that you enjoy them.'

The ballads drifted to an end, and Regan realised that she had been waiting in the apartment for over an hour.

Somehow, it hadn't seemed that long. She put on some moody jazz, and turned up the volume.

Placing her empty glass on the bar, she yielded to nervous curiosity and practical necessity and wandered down the hall to find the bathroom. It was as luxurious as the rest of the apartment, boasting a multi-head shower and an oval sunken bath almost twice the size of the entire bathroom back at the flat. Big, fluffy towels warmed on a heated towel-rail, and to Regan's amusement the toilet seat was also kept at a cosy temperature! Every conceivable toiletry a guest could require was thoughtfully provided, including—she discovered when she opened one of the drawers—a selection of various brands of tampons and condoms, nestled side by side in ironic juxtaposition.

She couldn't resist peeping into the half-open doors further down the hall to discover an office, two huge single bedrooms and, at the far end, an even bigger room with a sprawling king-sized bed which looked, to Regan's magnified awareness, as if it would sleep an army.

Most definitely the master bedroom, she decided, backing out...but not before she had noticed the black silk sheets, the tubular wooden slats on the teak bed-head and ends, unnervingly reminiscent of prison bars, and the vast mirror on the wall opposite the bed.

At least it wasn't fixed on the ceiling! she thought as she hurried back to the bar, wondering what she would do if 'Monsieur' turned out to be seriously kinky.

She diluted another icy vodka with a splash of tonic. She still wasn't entirely confident that she could handle a normal man's basic requirements, let alone satisfy one who demanded a performance artist in bed. But Pierre had said that the apartment was designed for use by a number of corporate executives, she reminded herself, in which case the master bedroom was generic, and not the personalised domain of the current occupant.

In fact, she thought, looking around the living area with a more critical gaze, there were no personal touches that she could see in the whole apartment. Like a plush hotel suite, or a photograph in an interior design magazine, it was sterile of private clutter. Unlike a permanent residence there were no books, photographs, knick-knacks or stray possessions to give any clue to the character of the present occupier.

When she tired of mooching around she absently kicked off her shoes and curled up on the wide, squashy cushions of the couch, sipping her drink, nibbling snacks and closing her eyes to soak up the music. She had almost dozed off when, coinciding with the end of the jazz disc, Regan heard the distinctive closing clunk of a heavy door and a rumbling exchange of masculine voices.

She leapt up from the couch, almost tripping over in her haste, smoothing down her dress and then her hair, unconsciously biting on her lower lip as she looked towards the entranceway. The voices faded briefly to a murmur and then became more distinct, Pierre's and one other…deeper and more staccato, edged with a weary impatience.

Suddenly Regan realised that she was curling her stockinged toes into the thick carpet, and she looked desperately around for her discarded high heels. She scooped them up and was hopping on one leg, still cramming the first shoe on her foot, when a living cliché came sauntering down the stairs.

He was tall, dark and handsome, wide-shouldered and lean-hipped, and he moved with the fluidity of an athlete.

Regan was stricken. She had gone from the ridiculous to the sublime in the space of a few hours!

This was going to turn out to be another nerve-shattering case of mistaken identity, she just *knew* it! Her whole mad plan had been doomed from the start.

He couldn't *possibly* be the man she had been waiting for; he was simply too unbelievably perfect!

CHAPTER THREE

'ALLOW me...'

Regan hadn't realised that she had dropped her other shoe until he stooped to pick it up.

'Uh, thank you...' she faltered, still balanced like a stork on her bare foot, stunned by the impact of his appearance.

Close up, the new arrival wasn't as classically handsome as he had first appeared. But he was certainly tall—over six feet—and his black suit and midnight-blue shirt and tie accentuated his dark colouring. His raven hair was thick and well-shaped, springing back from a slight widow's peak to brush his collar at the back. He was somewhere in his mid-thirties, she guessed, and already carrying a tiny trace of grey at his narrow temples.

There was intelligence in his gaze and cynicism in the hard cast of his features—a gambler's face, tense and watchful but betraying little of his own thoughts.

His eyes, which she had somehow expected to be also dark, were a light, penetrating steely-grey, slightly hooded under their heavy lids, and his stern Roman nose was framed by prominent cheekbones and a granite jaw. For such an athletic-looking man his skin was surprisingly pale and fine-grained, except on his lower cheeks and upper lip where it was roughened by a blue-black growth that was well beyond a five o'clock shadow.

Regan had to look a long, long way up at him, and as he inclined his head to meet her curious gaze she noticed the tracery of scars writhing up the left side of his lean throat and licking up under his jaw: the unmistakable scars of an old burn. To leave such a permanent stamp the injury must have been serious, and agonisingly painful.

So...he was damaged too—only his scars were on the outside...

Regan's eyes flickered down to the flimsy black shoe cupped in his large hand as she fought to reject the dangerous rush of empathy. She saw that his hands, too, bore evidence of scarring, but it was absurd to think that a man like him would ever want, or need, her sympathy.

'I—I took them off,' she explained breathlessly, lowering her shod foot to the floor and transferring her weight to it, going on tiptoe with the other to maintain stability.

He smiled at her redundant comment, a slow curve of his well-defined mouth that made her wobble on her uneven perch.

'So I see,' he murmured on a light, teasing note that was totally at odds with his air of hard-bitten cynicism and the hooded wariness of his eyes.

His stroking thumb measured the length of the delicate spike heel in his hand. 'Were they hurting you?'

His voice was deep and rasping, the husky edge abrading her senses like velvet sandpaper.

'No—I—I was just lying down...'

He arched his graceful brows and she was aghast to feel herself blush as she was visited with a sudden mental image of herself languishing nude on black silk sheets, like a slave girl awaiting the arrival of her lord and master.

'On the *couch*,' she firmly emphasised, her mouth unknowingly prim.

'Of course,' he agreed, the quicksilver amusement in his penetrating eyes making her wonder whether he could read her skittish mind. She went hot all over. Naive she might be, but surely she wasn't *that* transparent?

She tossed her head, rejecting the appalling notion, and

adopted a pose of haughty confidence which came immediately under assault.

'May I?'

Without waiting for an answer he knelt on the white carpet and encircled the ankle of her stockinged foot with lean fingers, tugging lightly to lift it from the floor.

Regan squeaked as she teetered off balance on her spindly heel, and grabbed at his shoulders to stay upright. Even through the padding of expensive fabric she could feel the shifting layers of solid muscle.

'What are you *doing*?' she gasped, wondering if he was some kind of weird foot-fetishist. 'Oh...'

She watched him slide her shoe back onto her foot, wiggling it from side to side to ease the fit. 'Thank you...you needn't have bothered,' she mumbled, embarrassed.

He tipped his head back, making no effort to rise. 'I enjoyed it,' he said, meeting her wide-eyed gaze, his fingers still lightly encircling her fine-boned ankle. 'You have very pretty feet. And legs...' he added, brushing his fingers gently up her calf to linger in the sensitive hollow at the back of her knee.

Regan stiffened as a violent tingle shot from her toes to her groin. Her heart beat furiously in her chest and her breathing quickened. She was no longer in any doubt. This was it. This was *him*. 'Thank you,' she said again, hoping that she didn't look as flustered as she felt.

'I'm sorry you had such a long wait. I hope you weren't too bored.' Having thoroughly disconcerted her with his Prince Charming act, he rose slowly back to his full height. Regan felt as if he was surveying every inch of her on the way up, and her body prickled with awareness, her eyes darkening and her nostrils flaring at the warm, spicy male scent that rose from his unbuttoned jacket.

'Pierre tells me that your name is Eve.'

She nodded, her eyelashes fluttering nervously at his

towering proximity. Being short, she was used to men looming over her, but she wasn't used to feeling such an acute sense of feminine self-awareness.

Unlike Pierre, he didn't display even a flicker of scepticism. 'How appropriate,' he said, capturing her hand and raising her knuckles briefly to his lips. 'In that case you can call me Adam.'

'Your name is Adam?' she repeated, jolted by the brush of his warm mouth into forgetting that the last thing she wanted to do was make an issue out of their names. Who would have thought one innocuous kiss on the back of her hand could feel so flagrantly erotic?

'One of them,' he smoothly conceded, stretching the coincidence. He lowered, but did not release her captive hand. 'So, here we are, Adam and Eve in a garden of delights...and this time there's not a serpent in sight.'

No serpent, just a worm who had finally turned! thought Regan, rescued from her confusion by a stirring of the wicked sense of humour which had lately been all but smothered out of existence.

'I'm sorry Cleo had to cancel,' she lied, sliding her tingling fingers slowly out of his hand, her fingernails scraping deliberately across his relaxed palm, crossing the faint ridge of a scar. 'I hope you aren't too disappointed.' She followed up her words by tilting her head so that her glossy locks slipped against her soft cheek, and giving him what she hoped was a brazen, woman-of-the-world smile.

A faintly arrested expression crossed his face. 'Every cloud has a silver lining,' he murmured, looking from the curve of her mouth to the glimpse of delicate earlobe, bare of ornamentation, to the turbulent depths of her violet eyes, shimmering with defiant excitement.

'And into every life a little rain must fall,' she responded vaguely, distracted by the darts of electricity zinging along her nerves into trotting out another of her mother's irritating maxims.

His lips quirked. 'Are you talking about Cleo's life, or mine?' His voice dropped to an insinuating growl. 'You're not planning to rain on my parade, are you, Eve?'

She wasn't quite sure of his meaning, but judging from his tone it had to be indecent. She touched her tongue to her upper lip. Witty sexual repartee was not exactly her forte.

She blundered on with the cryptic analogy. 'A man like you is always prepared for any eventuality. I'm sure you come equipped with your own umbrella.'

'A whole drawerful of them,' he agreed blandly. For some reason that made her remember what she had seen in the bathroom. No...surely they weren't talking about *contraception*?

Were they?

Whatever the topic of conversation, she was *not* going to ruin her image by blushing again!

'You look tired,' she blurted, seizing on the truth as the perfect diversionary tactic. She had noticed the faint blue tinge to the pale skin under his eyes, and the subtle tautness around his mouth and jaw that suggested a stern measure of control, and now she identified the lazy burr that had entered his tone. He was a man who concealed his fatigue well—as he probably instinctively hid any form of weakness.

'It's been a rough day. But don't worry, I'm rapidly getting my second wind,' he promised drily. He shot his cuff and glanced at his no-nonsense steel watch. 'I know it's late, and we may not get there for cocktails, but we can still make the banquet. If you'll just give me a few minutes to change...'

He had thought she was complaining! 'Oh, no—I didn't

mean—er Y-you don't have to rush—' she protested, laying a restraining hand on his elbow as he turned away.

All his former wariness had returned, and his smile was sharp with cynical understanding as he looked over his shoulder at her. 'Nonsense. You came here expecting to attend an elegant party at the most exclusive restaurant in town and I don't intend to deprive you of the pleasure,' he soothed.

Regan ignored his words in favour of his tone. He *was* tired, but he was resigned to going out because it was part of the unwritten bargain, and he was obviously a man who strictly honoured his obligations, however tiresome.

'I really don't mind if we go out to dinner or not,' she said, her hand tightening on the fabric of his suit.

'Really?' He turned back, but it was clear that he didn't believe her. He thought her a clone of the worldly Cleo—a selfish little cat who was out to milk their bargain for everything she could get.

'I'm not very hungry, anyway,' she told him, letting her hand drop. 'An expensive meal would be totally wasted on me. I think I ate too many of Pierre's wonderful canapés,' she explained ruefully.

There was a tiny pause as he studied her expression. 'So you would be quite content if I asked him to prepare a light meal for us here, instead,' he said slowly.

'I actually don't think I could manage anything at all,' she confessed, her earlier appetite having been swallowed up by the tension of meeting him. 'Whereas you probably need something substantial after your tough day...'

'But you're happy to keep me company while *I* eat...'

What did he think, that she would sulk and pout because he wanted to eat and she didn't? 'Of course.'

'And we'll join the party afterwards...'

'We don't have to do that, either, if you don't feel like going out. Unless, of course, there's some reason that you need to be seen making an appearance there,' she added hurriedly when his eyes narrowed, taking on a new and disturbing intensity.

'So…what you're suggesting is that we not leave the apartment at all?'

His soft-voiced drawl made Regan's knees go weak as she realised the full implications of her impulsive offer. If they didn't go out, then there would be nothing, and no one, to distract them from the *real* purpose of the evening. No way to hide from the consequences of her own actions.

'You're willing to forgo the excitement of a night on the town because *I've* had a rough day?' he continued in that same tone of silken curiosity.

She grasped her courage and opted for honesty. 'I expect that I'll have all the excitement I can handle right here,' she confessed, her wry words provoking him into a deep, purring laugh.

'Both kind *and* flattering—the perfect companion after a hard day at the office! I look forward to finding out how many other virtues you possess.'

Regan basked in an unexpected thrill of accomplishment. She had captivated his jaded interest—made him laugh. Maybe this was going to be easier than she had thought. After all, unlike her husband, this man *wanted* her to be sexy and seductive!

'If you were expecting a virtuous woman, you're going to be severely disappointed.' She flirted up at him through her lowered lashes.

He took her chin between his thumb and forefinger and tilted it until her eyelashes flew wide. 'No, I don't think so,' he mused, looking deep into her slumberous eyes. He brushed the pad of his thumb across her mouth, causing it to quiver and part, and then pressed firmly against her plump lower lip. She gave a little gasp as the tip of her tongue tasted the saltiness of his skin.

He misunderstood her tiny flinch. 'Don't worry, I'm not smearing your lipstick...it appears to have worn off.'

His tolerant humour made it obvious that he was used to women whose looks were their stock-in-trade.

Regan's eyebrows crumpled at the dent to her glamorous self-image. She had never thought to recheck her lipstick. 'It must have gone to garnish the canapés,' she laughed huskily, to disguise her chagrin. 'I'll put some more on while you're talking to Pierre about dinner—'

'No. Don't bother...' The pressure of his thumb stopped her words in her mouth. 'I like the nude look. I like the contrast between the sultry seduction of your elaborate eye make-up and the soft, pink innocence of your mouth.' And, as if that wasn't erotic enough to take her breath away, he added casually, 'Besides, I don't like the taste of lipstick.'

He took away his thumb and she swayed slightly, thinking that he was going to suit his actions to his words, but instead of following up his claim with a kiss he said indulgently, 'So how about fixing me a drink while I go and see Pierre about dinner? Whisky—on the rocks. The eight-year-old Scotch, if you please...'

Regan's hands were still trembling as she uncapped the Scotch and poured his drink, clashing the neck of the bottle against the squat crystal glass.

She ordered herself to calm down. They had the whole evening ahead of them...of course he didn't want to rush things. He was a highly civilised man. He wanted to unwind from his busy day first, to be amused and entertained in undemanding company. As Cleo had loudly insisted— this wasn't prostitution. And Adam had just proved her right with his willingness to do what his escort wanted rather than exercise his own preference. The message was that Regan was here to enjoy herself, not simply to provide raw sex on command...

When she turned from the bar her heart jumped to find

that Adam was already back, lounging on the couch, his
long legs splayed, his head tipped back against the pale
cushions, exposing his scarred throat as he gazed up at the
ceiling. He must have moved as silently as a cat. He had
shed his jacket and tie, the subtle sheen of his dark blue
shirt catching the light where his arms stretched along the
back of the couch. His collar was unbuttoned, and as she
moved closer she could see a drift of dark hair revealed by
the narrow V of his open shirt.

The ice cubes tinkled against the glass in her hand and
he rolled his head to one side and lazily watched her ap-
proach. In spite of the relaxation of his big body, Regan
wasn't fooled into thinking that his brain was clouded by
his fatigue. His eyes, though heavy-lidded, weren't in the
least bit drowsy as she offered him his drink.

He shifted his torso, dropping his right hand to rest near
his hip, but made no attempt to reach for the glass. After
a moment of dithering uncertainty she stepped between his
splayed knees to bend over and place his drink directly into
his hand.

His fingers flexed around the glass, momentarily trapping
hers against the slippery surface, and when she lifted her
head enquiringly she saw that his eyes weren't on her face.
They were level with the plunging front of her dress, where
her small, unconfined breasts, rounded almost to voluptu-
ousness by gravity, crowded up against the edge of the
deeply scooped neckline.

Trapped in her provocative pose, Regan was shocked to
feel her nipples tighten and begin to rub against the material
with every indrawn breath, as if beckoning his attention.

'You're not wearing a bra.' He voiced his intimate discovery, lifting his other hand to languidly trace a finger
around her curving neckline, careful not to touch the
creamy swells of flesh, only the seam of fabric against
which they strained. He took a sip of his drink as he did

so, allowing her captured fingers to slip away from the glass.

Deprived of the excuse to flaunt her modest charms in his face, Regan had to force herself to move. All he'd had to do, she thought, was tuck his finger into that edge and he would have been stroking her aching breasts...

'I—I'm so small I don't usually have to,' she said, her head throbbing with blood as she straightened reluctantly within the corral of his strong thighs.

'The best things come in small packages,' he murmured, letting his fingers trail down her bare arm, and then drift lightly over her hip and flank to the sensitive back of her knee, which he had earlier caressed with such electrifying effect.

'Stockings or pantyhose?' he wondered, plucking gently at the silky sheer black nylon.

Regan's tongue felt thick in her mouth. 'Stockings.'

Since she'd been widowed she had discovered a simple economy: it was cheaper to mix and match pairs of stockings than to buy pantyhose that might have to be discarded because of a ladder in one leg. But tonight it hadn't been economy dictating her choice of underwear.

'And, let me guess...black lace suspenders?'

She blushed at his gentle mockery. It seemed like such a ridiculous cliché, and yet the garter belt had made her feel wickedly sexy when she had been clipping it onto her silky stockings. She had bought the lacy black underwear on her second wedding anniversary, in a vain attempt to inject some excitement into her marriage bed. Of course, she hadn't known at the time that Michael's excitement was reserved for his busty blonde mistress!

Holding her rosy-cheeked gaze, Adam smoothed his spread hand slowly back up over the hem of her skirt and across the front of her thigh until he encountered the betraying outline of her suspender, pressing lightly to imprint it on his palm.

'Anything else?'

All her attention was concentrated on his hand on her leg.

'I beg your pardon?'

He took another swallow of whisky, watching her over the silvery rim. 'I asked if you were wearing anything else?'

She licked her lips. 'You mean a-apart from my dress?' she said huskily.

'I mean *under* your dress,' he clarified, removing his hand, but leaving behind its heated brand on her thigh.

Her eyes widened and she nodded jerkily. What kind of woman didn't wear panties when she went out, for goodness' sake? What if she got knocked over in the street, or was ambushed by a freak gust of wind? The potential for embarrassment was enormous. Even Lisa, who was an ardent minimalist, wore tanga briefs to cover the bare essentials!

'Black lace?'

She nodded again, riveted by the breathtaking boldness of that pantherish stare. He sipped his whisky and she had a strong premonition that what he was planning to say next was in the nature of a challenge.

'Would you take them off for me, if I asked you to?'

The air was sucked from her lungs and a molten wave of heat scorched through her veins.

'Y-You mean…here? *Now?*'

He tilted his head. 'Have I shocked you?'

Senseless.

Regan was furious. She'd thought she had been doing so well! And now he had flung down this outrageous gauntlet.

There was a faint smile on his face as he waited to see what she would do next, and to Regan the hint of mocking detachment in his regard was an added insult. She had a lowering suspicion that he wouldn't be surprised if she melted in a puddle of stammering embarrassment—that he had seen through her sophisticated charade to the nervous little mouse beneath.

No! She wasn't going to be shocked by his indecent proposal. Wasn't this precisely why she had come here—to play adult games, to experiment, to explore beyond the limits of her own experience? To celebrate her freedom from the tyranny of lies by flinging open the doors on her sequestered sexuality?

Aware of the danger she was courting, Regan was gripped by a powerful urge to shake up that infuriating masculine self-assurance…to pay him back, shock for shock. It struck her quite forcibly that, in spite of the explicit sexual threat that Adam represented, she was less afraid now than she had been all evening.

So… Adam wanted to see how far she could be pushed, did he? Well, now was the time to show him that she was more than equal to his game. Maybe if she had been more keen to indulge in sexual role-playing during their marriage then her husband would have been less keen to stray—except that Michael had never encouraged his loving wife to be anything other than strictly conventional in bed.

Conventional and boring!

Without a word Regan reached up under her skirt and hooked her shaking thumbs into the high-cut sides of her bikini panties.

Adam's face was suddenly wiped clean of all expression and he moved with lightning swiftness, his thighs tensing as he leaned abruptly forward to clamp a preventive hand on her forearm.

'I'm sorry…I was teasing you. I apologise for my lack of finesse,' he said, coolly snatching his gauntlet back out of her reckless grasp. 'I'd hate to spoil our evening by rushing pleasures that are better savoured. I'm afraid the potent combination of a sensuous woman and an excellent Scotch temporarily overwhelmed my self-control—not to mention my good manners,' he added, with just the right touch of rueful self-derision. He settled back with his whisky, looking up at her with carefully modified solemnity.

Smooth-talking devil! He might have been only teasing, but he had been in full control of all his faculties. He had been testing her compliance.

Pumped for action, Regan was tempted to ignore his glib apology and go ahead with her daring act of defiance. However, he had just referred to her as a sensuous woman, and for that delicious compliment she was almost willing to forgive him. If he had called her beautiful she wouldn't have believed him, but to be sensuous a woman didn't have to have model-girl looks. Beauty was only skin-deep, whereas sensuality was innate—and therefore infinitely more desirable as far as Regan was concerned.

She reluctantly removed her hands and ran them slowly up and down the side-seams of her dress, deliberately wiggling her hips as she smoothed the rumpled fabric back into place. It felt wild and wanton, stroking herself like this in front of him, but it was the kind of thing that a sensuous woman *would* do—inviting a man to share her feminine appreciation of her own body.

He watched, his face softening with a return of his former amusement, but this time it was laced with a measure of wry respect.

'Why don't you join me?' he murmured, intrigued by the hint of shy excitement in her slinky self-absorption.

'Thank you, I will…' she purred, caught up in her performance, her eyes glowing with smug triumph as she sank onto the empty cushions beside him. The couch was long enough to take his full length—and wide enough for an orgy, she thought, nervously.

'I meant in a drink,' he explained, toasting her with his glass.

'Oh…' Her sultry look dissolved. 'I did have a vodka and tonic around here somewhere…' She frowned vaguely about.

'Forget it. Just go ahead and help yourself to another,' Adam advised with the careless ease of a man who never had to worry about a budget—for alcohol or anything else. Lounging at his ease, he obviously expected her to play hostess while Pierre was occupied in the kitchen.

She thought she had probably infused enough alcohol into her system as it was, but a drink would give her some occupation for her nervous hands.

She stood up, ultra-conscious of her lack of grace as her narrow heels tilted awkwardly into the thick pile of the carpet and almost tipped her sideways into his lap. 'Shall I freshen yours, too?' she asked, to distract him from her clumsiness.

'No, it's fine,' he said, swirling the contents of his glass. 'You pour a mean Scotch.'

Regan shrugged with her hands. 'My father was a big whisky-drinker—' She bit her lip as she turned away, annoyed at her slip. She knew the cheap rot-gut that had killed her father by the time she was ten had little in common with the smooth, expensive, aromatic spirit that Adam savoured.

'And your husband? What about him?'

Her body stiffened as she swung back to face his grating accusation.

'My what?'

He caught at her left hand, lifting it to the light so that they both could see the faint band of pale skin on her ring finger. He immediately let it drop, as if contaminated by her touch.

'Are you married?' he demanded harshly.

She hesitated. Just what kind of man was she dealing with? 'What if I said yes?'

The light grey eyes hardened to cold steel. 'Then I'd politely show you the door. And Derek would cease to be part of my acquaintance. He knows my opinion on the subject: I don't sleep with other men's wives. And I despise cheating and deception—*No-one* gets a second chance to breach my trust. So if you *are* married tell me now, before this goes any further, because I make a very bad enemy...'

Regan was stunned by the ruthless force behind his pronouncement. He possessed the will, the wealth and the power to protect his personal honour, and wouldn't hesitate to use those weapons to threaten and punish anyone who sought to compromise it in pursuit of their own interests.

'I'm not married,' she declared huskily, her curiosity more than satisfied.

Unfortunately, his suspicion was too sharp to be easily blunted by the belated admission.

'But you *were*,' he rapped out. 'Divorced?'

If she hadn't been so naive for so long she might have been able to say yes with dignity. As things stood, there was little honour in being Michael's widow.

She shook her head and looked down, disturbed to find herself twisting the non-existent ring on her finger.

'Widowed. Mi—my husband was killed in a car crash.'

There was a brief, splintering silence.

'I'm sorry.'

Her chin jerked up at the deep gentleness of his tone, her cheeks stinging as if he had reached out and slapped her. The cold steel had gone from his eyes, to be replaced by a smoky speculation that made her angry heart burn. She didn't want tenderness, dammit! All she wanted from him was one night of simple, uncomplicated lust.

'Don't be.'

His eyes narrowed at the clipped command.

'Like that, was it?' he mused, still with that threatening undertone of softness.

She raked her fingers through her hair, and flicked the ends over her shoulder in a gesture half-nervous, half-defiant. 'You can't begin to imagine what it was like,' she said with a tight smile. 'And I'd rather you didn't bother.'

'How long ago did it happen?'

She tossed him a frustrated look. She could guess what he was thinking—he was wondering whether she was acting out some psychological trauma associated with her marriage.

With a vengeance!

Her eyes flashed. 'Long enough.'

Eight months. Long enough for her to have found out why Michael had insisted on handling all their joint finances. He had spent their savings, run up credit card debts, mortgaged the house and taken out loans for which, as his next of kin and inheritor of his estate, she was liable. The absence of a will had compounded the legal problems, and only after months of trying to straighten out the chaotic financial tangle her lawyer had informed her that there was little left to inherit.

And two weeks ago she had finally discovered why.

Two weeks ago she had received a tearful visit from Michael's long-term mistress, the earthy, voluptuous Cindy...and his three-and-a-half-year-old son.

Her last remaining shred of respect for Michael had vanished as she had been forced to face the degrading truth that for the entire duration of their marriage her husband had been living an expensive double life. One that she, all unknowingly, had helped finance!

Well, tonight she would have her revenge.

Tonight she wasn't going to be the sweet, understanding little woman, bravely swallowing her pride and doing what was expected of her.

Tonight *she* was going to be the ruthless user, the unrepentant sinner...

CHAPTER FOUR

'So you don't miss having a husband?'

Like a hole in the head, Regan wanted to snap. Instead, she channelled her anger into another emotion.

'I miss...*certain things* about being married...' She tossed Adam a suggestive smile and swung back over to the bar. Conscious of his eyes levelled on her back, she relaxed her shoulders and moved with an exaggerated sway of her hips, the way she had seen Lisa move on the catwalk.

Drink in hand, she strolled back with that same, slinky roll and crossed her legs as she sat down, letting her skirt ride up above her knees as far as it liked.

'Would you like me to do that for you?' she offered, as he eased a hand across the back of his neck, digging his fingers into the tense muscle.

'You do massage?'

'I'm not a qualified masseur or anything,' she said innocently, 'but I'm sure I could give you a rub that would ease some of your tension.'

'I think having your hands on my body is more likely to increase rather than decrease my tension,' he said, with the faint smile that turned her insides to marshmallow.

She cleared her throat of a tiny obstruction. In the background she was vaguely aware of Pierre, moving to and fro from the kitchen to the table. 'So...what sort of things do you normally do to unwind after a hard day at the office?' she asked.

From his bland expression she knew he was going to tease her again. 'Well...I find flirting with a warmly receptive woman very relaxing.'

45

'Then you should soon be a positive puddle of contentment,' she responded, equally bland.

His quick grin was white and wolfish. 'I already feel myself melting. And what do you like to do to relax, Eve?'

'Oh, read, sew, cook…' she said demurely. She lowered her lashes and slowly lifted them again. 'Make love…'

'Interesting. I usually find that the act of sex has the opposite effect,' he murmured, topping her with stunning ease. 'I don't feel in the least relaxed when I'm inside a woman's body. I'm all edgy and agitated, and every muscle feels explosively hot and tight with urgency…' He paused to take a swallow of whisky, enjoying the way her violet eyes widened and the pulse at the base of her bare throat kicked up a storm. 'But perhaps the feelings are very different for a woman…'

Regan hoped not! She mastered the impulse to throw herself on top of him and demand that he demonstrate right there and then.

She gave a blasé shrug of her slender shoulders instead. 'Men and women aren't so very different—'

'Honey, if you think that, then you must have skipped human biology in high school,' he interrupted drolly.

In fact her mother *had* removed her from class whenever there had been a danger she might be contaminated by sex education disguised as legitimate learning.

'I took Classics rather than Sciences,' she retaliated. 'But I meant in terms of having equal sexual needs and desires.'

'Equal but different,' he agreed. 'I don't suppose my sexual fantasies are the same as yours.'

He sounded so smugly certain she immediately wanted to take him down a peg or two. 'Which is not to say yours are any better than mine!'

He almost choked on the dregs of his whisky as a chuckle rumbled up from his chest. 'If I show you mine will you show me yours?'

Her blank response prompted him to continue. 'Didn't you ever play doctors and nurses as a kid?'

'I was an only child.'

'And? Surely there was some chubby little charmer in the neighbourhood who suggested disappearing into the nearest wardrobe with his play-stethoscope and handy torch?'

'If he had, he'd have found himself without a head.'

'So you were an aggressive, assertive little girl?' he speculated, looking deeply intrigued.

'I was very biddable and angelic,' she said primly, using a straight face to imply that her truth was actually an outrageous lie. 'But my mother was extremely vigilant where the seven deadly sins were concerned.'

'Thereby not giving you much of a chance to be anything else,' he guessed with uncomfortably swift perception.

'I'm sure I still have my trusty halo here somewhere,' she said, delicately patting her fingertips down the side of her dress.

'Somewhat tarnished by now, I suppose?' he drawled, his gaze following the taunting trail.

'Oh, I take it out every now and then and give it a good polish,' she said, exhilarated by her newfound ability to hold her own against his quick wit.

'And groom your golden wings?'

'No wings,' she dimpled, 'but I do have a pitchfork in my other dress.'

'Ahh…a woman of dangerous contradictions. I see my first act should not have been to kiss your hand but to pat you down for concealed weapons.'

She spread her arms in graceful offering. 'Feel free to do so now; I won't hold it against you.'

'Not even if I beg?' As a laugh gurgled in her throat his eyes flicked across to the elevated dining area, where Pierre was placing a bottle of Krug champagne into a silver ice-bucket on the table, next to a covered chafing dish. He drained his glass and set it down. 'It looks as if Pierre has served up. Shall we?'

Two elegant place-settings were angled next to each other at the head of the oval table; the overhead down-lights were dimmed, and the dancing flame of a slender candle was dully reflected in the burnished surface of the wood. A sheaf of the palest pink roses in a fan-shaped hand-blown vase complemented the oval white place-mats gleaming with silver and crystal.

Adam politely said something about washing his hands, and followed Pierre briefly into the kitchen. When he returned Regan was still standing behind the chair at the head of the oval table, her hands balled by her sides, her face mantled with a light flush that made him eye her thoughtfully. As he approached she drew back the chair and invited him to be seated with a tilt of her head.

'Usurping my gentlemanly duties?' he murmured, accepting the courtesy with a lazy smile, and Regan picked up the white damask napkin from beside his plate and snapped out the starched folds to drape it across his lap. 'When I told Pierre that we wouldn't need him for the rest of the evening, I envisaged that *I* would be waiting on *you*,' he added.

'I thought you might feel in the mood to be pampered,' said Regan, unfolding her fist and casually laying another item on top of his napkin.

He glanced down, and she was elated to see the ripple of shock glaze his features. His eyelids drooped and the hard jaw slackened and it was several exhilarating heartbeats before he regained sufficient mastery of his expression to hike up a mocking eyebrow.

'Misplaced something, Eve?' He lifted the wisp of black lace above the level of the table, dangling it from his crooked finger.

'Not at all,' she drawled. His eyes were irresistibly drawn to the outline of her hips and she made the most of it, sliding her bottom onto the padded chair with provocative slowness and squirming to make herself comfortable.

'Tease!' His soft accusation was redolent with masculine appreciation as he watched the performance.

Her dress slid against her bare skin and the slight coolness between her legs made her feel dangerously vulnerable, especially when her knee brushed his under the table. She pressed her quivering thighs together, excited by her daring. It felt so good to be so thoroughly bad that she wondered why she hadn't tried it years ago.

He danced the swatch of lace on his crooked finger. 'Then what's this? Some form of nouvelle cuisine appetiser designed to stimulate my jaded palate?'

It was her turn to look glazed as he dropped the skimpy black panties onto his gold-rimmed white plate and picked up his fork to lightly stir the frothy lace.

'I must admit, they do look good enough to eat.' He twirled the fork into the silky fabric, winding it up as if it was an exotic form of pasta.

'Adam—no!' she squeaked, clapping her hands to her mouth to contain her appalled laughter. She hadn't expected such an obvious sophisticate to possess such a mischievous sense of humour.

He paused, looking wickedly crestfallen. 'You don't wear edible panties?' he asked.

She had seen them in novelty gift shops and thought them embarrassingly tacky. 'Certainly not!'

Her scandalised denial made his mouth twitch. 'Then I suppose I'll have to settle for whatever Pierre has rustled up,' he said, calmly plucking the panties off his fork and tucking them casually into his breast pocket. He lifted the domed lid of the chafing dish to reveal a fragrant pile of steaming stir-fried vegetables burnished with a sesame-flecked sauce. 'Will you have some?'

Regan tore her eyes away from the lace frothing out of his pocket. 'No, I don't think so…' She watched him heap a generous serving of the vegetables onto his plate. 'Are you a vegetarian?'

He shook his head as he poured Krug into two long-stemmed glasses of Edinburgh lead-crystal. 'I asked Pierre to prepare something that would digest easily. I know a meal is considered the conventional prelude to seduction, but I don't think one should make love on an overly full stomach. Do you?'

The glass of champagne he handed her nearly slipped through her fingers. 'I—I never really thought about it…'

'You mean you usually just act on your natural instincts—I like that in a woman.' His approving look was transferred to his food as he savoured it with all his senses. 'Mmm….this is good. Here. Try a taste.' He held out a piece of glazed carrot on his fork and Regan automatically leaned forward to take it in her mouth.

'Good?' he asked, tempting her with another offering, this time of succulently crisp green pepper.

The sticky sauce was sweet, yet tart, and hotly spicy on the tongue. 'Scrumptious,' she admitted, her eyes half closing with bliss as he trailed the tines of his fork from her moisture-glossed lower lip. The gentle scraping against the soft pad of flesh sent a little shiver down her spine.

'Are you sure you won't have some?'

'Well…maybe a little.' She yielded to his culinary seduction, deciding that tonight no temptation was worth resisting.

As they ate Adam kept the conversation to light, entertaining subjects that rarely threatened to get too personal, but the look in his eyes was extremely personal and with every bite Regan was made more aware of the fact that he

was a man and she was a woman—and that he had her
panties in his pocket. Her daring tease had had the desired
effect, and Adam was making no secret of his gently sim-
mering arousal. He watched her mouth as she ate and her
eyes as she sipped at her champagne; he watched the way
her small hands balanced the solid silver cutlery and how
her throat rippled when she swallowed; he seemed to find
special fascination in the delicate skin that stretched across
her collarbone and the movement of her breasts against her
dress as she gestured and spoke.

Unused to being the focus of such concentrated masculine attention, Regan found herself increasingly responsive
to the charged atmosphere created by his cool wit and hot,
knowing looks. Just looking at him was like plugging directly into an electrical circuit—her whole body hummed
with a pleasurable buzz of nervous anticipation. She noticed
the easy flexibility in his strong wrists as his scarred hands
tipped the heavy champagne bottle, the sexy lines that
amusement carved in his taut cheeks and the muscle that
jumped in his jaw when he mentally withdrew to brood on
some private thought.

She was so caught up in her heightened self-awareness
that when Adam finally pressed his napkin against his
mouth all she could think of was how it would feel if he
pressed *her* to those firm lips...

She found out when he suddenly threw the rumpled napkin down on his empty plate and with a rough sound of
impatience reached over to jerk her out of her chair, tum-
bling her across his lap.

'And now you can make good on that promise,' he
growled, supporting her slender back with one powerful
arm as his other hand cupped her squirming hip, forcing
her soft bottom against the bunched muscles of his thighs.

Her startled cry of alarm had made her breathless. 'What
promise?' she gasped, her head falling back against his

shoulder as she recognised she was helpless against his
strength, even had she wanted to struggle...

'This one,' he rasped, silking his hand up under her
dress, over the tops of her stockings, to stroke the satiny
skin of her inner thighs, his fingertips drifting so close to
the core of her feminine heat that she felt the fierce electrical jolt of his imaginary penetration.

Regan instinctively snapped her legs together, her squeak
of shock smothered by his mouth coming hard down on
hers, plundering her senses with a ruthless expertise that
left her weak and panting.

He kissed her until she thought that her head was going
to explode and her heart accelerate out of her chest. This
was no coy flirtation—his forceful kisses were in brazen
earnest. And after a slightly clumsy start Regan abandoned
herself to his miraculous passion, splinters of delight cas-
cading through her senses. His tongue slid in and out of
her mouth, deftly stroking her in ways that made her twist
feverishly in his lap, seeking even more intimate contact,
sliding her arms around his neck and running her fingers
up the back of his scalp to sift through his luxuriant dark
hair, tugging at it in her eagerness to experience everything
he had to offer.

But it still wasn't enough—he was too controlled and
she needed more, much more—so she leaned hungrily into
his devouring kisses, using her teeth and tongue to encour-
age him to stop holding back, to be rougher, more reckless...

He refused to co-operate, and she ran a hand down the
side of his face, over his gritty jaw and down his flawed
throat to his open collar, where she ripped blindly at the
buttons to gain access to that tantalising strip of hair-
roughened chest. Under the dark mat of hair his skin felt
smooth and hot to her fingertips, and she curled her nails
into the resilient wall of flesh, revelling in the way his

muscles bunched and rippled at the warning prick of five tiny daggers.

He grunted, his knuckles digging into her soft flesh as he flexed the hand trapped between her clenched thighs, forcing it gradually higher until his thumb brushed against the soft nest of hair protecting her femininity.

He broke the kiss and her head fell back against his shoulder. He bit at her exposed throat and then suckled at the glowing red marks. 'You're so incredibly hot for me,' he rasped as her sultry need irradiated the torrid, enclosed space between her thighs, misting the tip of his thumb. 'So ready for me...'

Had there been an odd note of surprise in his gloating words? 'Isn't that what you wanted?' she managed threadily.

'What I want from a woman and what I get are not always the same thing,' he murmured, moving his thumb the infinitesimal distance to final contact and watching her violet eyes bloom with colour so vibrant and intense that it was beyond the palette of any artist. 'But you may be unique in that respect. You're not going to have to fake a thing with me, are you, Eve?' This time his purring voice was purely triumphant.

'You're hot for me, too,' she countered, flattening her hand over his steamy chest.

He bent and licked her mouth. 'Hot and hard,' he conceded in an inflammatory whisper, moving his hips so that she felt the explicit truth of his words rubbing against her bottom.

He continued to kiss her with the same, slow, teasing rhythm with which he controlled the delicate movements of his thumb. Only when he felt her quivering thighs relax and her hips begin to lift towards his tantalising touch did he withdraw his hand to cup her breast, his fingers finding and moulding the stiff nipple through the fine fabric, drawing it out to an exquisite peak of sensitivity.

'Adam…' Regan's protest was a soft moan as she squeezed her thighs together, trying to ease the burning ache created by the loss of his vital touch at the core of her femininity.

'Eve…' He said something else that she didn't hear over the thunderous roar of her blood, and when his arms braced, gently yet inexorably easing her away from his body, a brief battle ensued that left him smouldering with sensual amusement.

'I said…I think it's time we adjourned to the bedroom while we can both still walk,' Adam said, his hands firm on her narrow waist as he rose with her struggling figure and set her squarely on her feet. 'I'd prefer to finish this in the luxury and comfort of a well-sprung bed…wouldn't you?'

His smile was mildly taunting, as if he sensed how close she had been to ravishing him right there in his chair.

Finish this? What if she didn't want to finish it? What if she never wanted to relinquish this glorious feeling of voluptuous well-being?

'Shall we…?' He turned her gently in the direction of the bedroom and invited her company with a spurring little pat on the bottom that ended in a lingering caress.

In spite of her turmoil Regan remembered to snatch up her beaded bag as they passed the couch, hugging it to her fast-beating heart as she walked down the wide hall and into the big bedroom which she had found so intimidating. Someone had already been in to turn on the recessed lights and fold back the corner of the dark bedcover to display an inviting expanse of lustrous black silk. Pierre, setting up the final scene for seduction, thought Regan as she noticed how some of the lights were angled to pool on the bed, making it appear to float above the pale carpet.

Adam was emptying his trouser pockets, placing the contents on the top of a tall dresser. He flicked open the remaining buttons of his shirt and reached for a nearby switch on the wall, illuminating an adjoining bathroom that Regan had failed to notice earlier, so intent had she been on the bed.

'You won't mind if I take a shower first, to rinse off the grime of the day?' He stripped his shirt down his arms and tossed it onto a chair by the wall, her lacy panties still decorating the pocket.

He stretched unselfconsciously, enjoying the freedom of his own skin, and Regan lost any chance of making a polite reply.

His nipples were dark brown against the lightness of his skin, mounted on slabs of muscle which were covered by a thicket of dark silky hair flecked here and there with rare strands of silver. The scars that marked his throat ended in a shiny swirl just below his collarbone, the rest of him—as far as she could see—was well nigh perfect. His belly was flat, with hints of corrugated muscle that flexed and rippled along his front and sides when he lifted his arms. The hair on his chest formed an inverted triangle, narrowing abruptly to a thin, downy line that ended well above his indented navel. In the huge mirror on the far wall Regan could see the reflection of his long, lean, unblemished back. He had already started to unbuckle his plain black leather belt and her eyes dipped helplessly to the obvious thrust of his arousal against the expensive black fabric of his trousers.

He saw her looking and prowled over to cup her jaw. 'I'd ask you to join me, but one stroke of your soapy hands and I'm afraid I'd go off like a rocket,' he admitted frankly, 'and I have a rather more extended form of foreplay in mind. Besides—' he lowered his head to graze his mouth and nose along her cheek '—you already smell deli-

cious…that perfume you're wearing is the perfect aphrodisiac.' He nipped at her tender earlobe, making her shiver.
'If you like to play games in the water, how about we have
a Jacuzzi together later…?' He padded towards the open
bathroom door, pausing to tease her with an uplifted eyebrow. 'Wait for me?'

As if there could be any doubt that she would! thought
Regan shakily, listening to the sound of a shower being
turned on and the low buzz of a razor soon superseded by
the intermittent splash of water hitting a solid object. A
very solid, masculine column of flesh.

Regan hovered in the centre of the floor, wondering what
to do. Should she undress…or would he want to do that?
Did he expect her to be lying naked in bed when he returned, or did his notion of 'extended foreplay' require her
to be perched on the covers in a provocative pose? She
blinked dizzily at the thought and looked hastily around for
a distraction, hesitating as she caught sight of herself in the
mirror. Was that really her?

Her black dress looked somehow tighter, the neck lower
and the hem higher, than it had at home. Her black satin
hair was in tousled disorder, her mouth reddened and her
eyes as dark as bruises in her flushed face. She put a hand
to her throat and ran it down the front of the dress, over
her taut breasts and down to the bottom of her skirt. She
inched it up until the top of her stocking showed, and then
a strip of bare thigh. She bent her knee and looked sideways
at herself. No sign of a victim now—she was all vamp. She
had never looked nor felt so brazenly sexy in her life.

She let her hem fall and wandered over to the dresser,
trying not to strain her ears for noises from the bathroom.
Along with the heap of items from Adam's pocket—a scat-
ter of small change, a set of keys, a slim crocodile-skin
wallet—there was a silver-backed male brush and comb set
lying next to a small black leather case, the open zip of

which displayed a manicure kit. The only other item of a possibly personal nature was a long, narrow navy blue jeweller's box.

Her *reward*...?

The shower was still splashing erratically.

Regan put down her bag and picked up the velvet box. The lid was stiff and her fingers sweaty with nervous guilt as she forced it back on its hinges.

She sucked in a sharp breath. The thin tennis bracelet was lying on a bed of blue velvet, the tiny diamond chips a blaze of white ice under the overhead light. God knows how much such a thing had cost!

Regan snapped the box shut and hastily replaced it exactly as she had found it. If that was what Adam planned to give his lady of the evening, she didn't want him to know that she had been snooping. But...oh, God, how flattering to be considered worthy of such loveliness. She went soft inside at the thought of those strong, scarred hands fastening the delicate strand of diamonds around her wrist.

Except for her wedding and engagement rings Michael had never given her any jewellery. His birthday gifts to her had usually been small household appliances and her most romantic anniversary present had been a cookbook.

But there was nothing romantic about the receipt of this first gift of jewellery, either, Regan reminded herself fiercely. She mustn't fall into the trap of thinking there was anything personal involved. Just because the bracelet was beautiful that didn't make it in any way *meaningful*, to either herself or Adam. It wasn't the gift of a lover; it was hard, cold evidence of their transaction, that was all. The bracelet hadn't been bought with her specifically in mind— nor, probably, had Adam even selected it himself.

She picked up her evening purse and unzipped it, determined to bring herself firmly back to earth. Pushing aside the condom packet, which showed a distressing tendency to stick to her damp fingers, she drew out the little square box she was searching for and opened it. The elegant gold cufflinks inset with darkly grained New Zealand jade stared accusingly back at her. They had been extremely costly, but Regan had been frugal with the housekeeping money for a long time in order to secretly save up for something special for Michael's twenty-eighth birthday. But he had been killed a week before she could give them to him, and in the emotional turmoil that followed the cufflinks had lain forgotten in the pocket of a rarely worn jacket until she had rediscovered them a few days ago.

She *had* intended to sell them, but tonight it had seemed like poetic justice to use the pathetic evidence of her wasted love to buy her way out of any pangs of conscience about her sexual fling.

'What are you doing?'

Regan stuffed the box back into her bag and whirled around, suddenly registering the lack of sound from the bathroom behind her.

Her mouth went dry. Adam wasn't quite naked but the towel wrapped around his lean hips rode drastically low, and the end tucked into the folds over his right hip-bone seemed tantalisingly insecure. Here and there on his skin was a faint beading of moisture, as if he had been in too much of a hurry to dry himself properly, and the hair on his chest glistened as if the strands had been individually polished. As he walked towards her the towel parted on his right thigh with every stride, showing her a lithe strip of hair-dusted muscle.

'I—I was just getting these,' she improvised, holding up the packet of condoms as she pushed her bag onto the dresser.

He wrapped his hand around hers and plucked the packet from her fingers, tossing it on top of her purse, not taking his eyes off her flustered face. 'You won't need them.'

Her eyes widened as the breath swooped from her lungs, the clean, soapy scent of him clogging her nostrils. The light gleamed on his cheek, making his freshly shaven jaw look as smooth as polished silk.

'But you— But I—' She couldn't believe he would risk either a sexually transmitted disease or a pregnancy from their encounter—so what kind of sexual activity *did* he have in mind?

His mouth kinked in amusement at her nervous stutter. 'I mean, I prefer to use my own,' he explained.

'Oh.' Her relief was writ large in her eyes before a frown wrinkled her fringe. 'You don't trust me? What do you think—that I've been at them with a pin?'

'It has been known to happen,' he said mildly, and she realised that it wasn't her he mistrusted, but women in general...perhaps even *people* in general.

That made the insult a little easier to take—but not much. He had no way of knowing that she was the last woman to want to trap him into any extended responsibility for their one-night stand.

'You must have a very pessimistic outlook on life,' she told him.

'Well, right at this moment I'm extremely *op*timistic about the immediate future,' he said, fingering the strap of her dress as he looked down into her eyes. 'For instance...I have complete confidence in your ability to arouse me...' He pushed the strap off her shoulder and bent to nuzzle the tender crease where her arm met the upper swell of her breast.

There was a soft rustle and she felt his towel brush against her calf as it fell to the floor. He was now stark naked, and only inches away from her electrified body. Apart from Michael, Regan had never seen a naked adult male in the flesh...let alone aroused. She let her eyes fall to the level of his chest as he toyed with her other strap.

She didn't dare look down any further, in case she completely lost her nerve.

She lifted her hands and laid them tentatively against his chest and he gave a shuddering sigh, his breath hot against her smooth shoulder.

'Oh, yes…that's right…touch me—show me how good you are with your hands.…' He kissed the side of her throat and put his hands over hers, stroking them up and down his chest. She could feel his heart thudding and her palms grew hot with the friction from the thick growth of hair. When he let her hands go to cup her head and angle her mouth up to his she let her fingers settle on either side of his flat waist, gripping hard as he shifted his stance, making her vividly conscious of a blunt force nudging against the front of her skirt.

He kissed her as he had before, with a deep thoroughness that made her knees turn to water. Drowning in sensation, she closed her eyes and dug her fingernails into his waist and he laughed into her mouth.

'Little cat…'

His hands slipped down the slender line of her back and suddenly she could feel them warmly cupping her bare bottom under the rucked up skirt, stroking the downy plumpness, tracing the sensitive crease in a way that made her automatically clench her buttocks. He growled with approval, his hands tightening as he squeezed and kneaded, lifting her hips hard against him so that she couldn't avoid the thick roll of flesh thrusting into her belly, and bending his head to string a sting of moist kisses into her plunging neckline. Her eyes flew open and she could feel the heat pulse between her legs at the sight of his dark head moving against her breasts and the feel of his teeth through the snug fabric.

He backed her trembling legs towards the bed, and as he angled them across the room she glimpsed their reflection in the mirror and gasped—the side-on view of a big, naked man in a passionate embrace with a partly clad female was like a scene from an erotic movie, her bared bottom starkly pale against the folds of her black dress, his hands positioned with an explicit sexual intent that gave her a sharp thrill of anticipation.

He had paused in his uneven progress, following her mesmerised gaze.

'Do you like what you see, little Eve?' One hand drifted down her buttocks and they both watched it burrow between her thighs. 'Mmm, I see that you do,' he said, testing with a lingering finger as the woman in the mirror quivered and arched her back.

He spun her around so that she could no longer see the mirrored wall. 'But for now I want you to concentrate on *me*, not on *him*...'

For a sickening instant she thought that he was referring to Michael, then she realised that he was teasing her again. She had never been taught that sex could be fun.

'You can't be jealous of yourself!' she sparkled.

'Can't I?' he said, in the tone of a man who could be whatever the hell he wanted. 'You can't have us both, honey—it's him or me.'

'But he's such a hunk!' she pouted, pretending to peep around his elbow at his reflection.

His eyes narrowed warningly above his silky smile. 'You think so...?'

'Well...he's in much better shape than you are,' she said, walking her fingers daintily up his chest. She had reached a nipple and stopped to explore. 'He has much bigger muscles.'

'Bigger than this?' he growled, grabbing her dancing fingers and pulling them down to his groin. She gave a little squeak as he folded her hand around himself, stunned by the feel of the rigid shaft stroking against her palm as he undulated his hips. He felt as hard as steel, yet satiny soft and smooth as he slipped through her fingers, so hot that she could feel sympathetic perspiration breaking out all over her body. Her fingers felt too swollen for her skin, stiff and clumsy as she tried to be gentle, knowing from her self-defence classes that men were extremely sensitive to pressure in that part of their anatomy. To the sharp scent of soap was now added the potent, musky aroma of male desire.

'Too much for you to handle, Eve?' he taunted, hardening further under her featherlight fumbling. He picked up her other hand and enfolded snugly it around the base of his shaft. 'Here, why not use both hands…? And no need to treat me like spun glass—I won't break.'

She gulped, looking helplessly down at his captive manhood framed by her cupped hands, and the thick cloud of hair in his groin. All that throbbing power in her fragile grasp, she wondered…all that magnificent masculinity hers to command…

She contracted her fingers, unconsciously licking her lips, and a groan ripped from his chest. He gripped her by the shoulders, pulling her close so that her hands were crushed between them and the tips of her breasts scraped against his chest.

'Well, do you think I measure up?' he asked harshly as his body threatened to career out of his control.

'To what—the Empire State Building?' she said, striving to match his banter.

She felt his jolting laugh clear to the precious heaviness nestling hotly in her hands.

'I'm flattered you even mention us in the same breath, Honey, but speaking about comparing measurements…'

He reached around her back and she felt her zip give all the way down her spine and instinctively reached up to clutch at the loosening fabric over her breasts.

His groan of explicit regret as she released him made her blush, and she babbled defensively, 'I hope you're not expecting the pyramids here—I'm not very big...'

'So you told me earlier,' he murmured, tugging away her folded arms so that the dress slithered to her hips. 'Small and perfectly proportioned for your size,' he approved, as her rosy round breasts came into view, the pert nipples trembling with each shallow rise and fall of her ribcage. 'A very tempting little mouthful...'

And so it proved as he bent her back over his arm and cupped her breast, lifting it to his mouth so that he could lick at the dark pink crown, circling and flicking at it with his tongue until it ripened into a plum-red berry that he could nibble and suck with lusty pleasure before transferring his attention to its neglected twin. Wave after wave of delight crested through Regan's body as her dress slipped to the floor and was impatiently kicked away.

She wasn't even aware of moving, but the backs of her knees hit the side of the bed and she felt him dip and wrench away the covers with one hand an instant before she sprawled backwards onto the cool sheets, taking him with her. She squirmed underneath his heavy weight and he laughed exultantly, rolling with her into the middle of the wide bed, his thighs pushing heavily between hers as he pinned her to the slippery silk. He ran his hands down her stockinged legs and crouched back on his knees to flip off her dainty shoes before manacling her ankles and wrapping them around his lean flanks as he came back down on top of her, crushing his arousal against the moist thicket in the V of her body, shuddering with tension as he braced himself on bended elbows above her panting body.

'You're so beautifully responsive that you drive me wild,' he said hoarsely, cupping her head in his scarred hands. 'Look at me—I can't control myself. So much for my fine boasts about foreplay...'

Her violet eyes drank in the glorious sight of him—the dominant male, helpless in the grip of the passion that *she* had generated...

'Oh, Adam...' She knew then that the real gift she was taking away tonight was far more valuable than diamonds. This wonderful, sexy stranger had given her the confidence to be a woman again.

She arched her hips in an age-old invitation and raised her arms to pull him down to her hungry mouth. 'It's you I want, not your clinical expertise,' she told him in a sultry husk that carried the warm ring of truth. 'I'd rather have honest lust than a textbook demonstration of the Kama Sutra...'

His heavy-lidded eyes gleamed with richly sensual amusement as he succumbed to her steamy challenge, reaching down between them to where their bodies almost joined. 'Then, Eve, shall we open the gates of paradise...? And maybe what we find there will enable me to rise to the occasion and give you *both*...'

CHAPTER FIVE

'WELL, Lass, it won't be long now.'

Regan glanced in amusement at her employer, who was fidgeting in his eagerness to get to their destination.

'Next on the right!' The bullhorn bark belied his benign, roly-poly appearance, and she swiftly returned her attention to her driving.

Two months ago she wouldn't have had the confidence to chauffeur the big, expensive Jaguar, but since *That Night* she had discovered an adventurous spirit within herself which had encouraged her to believe that she could conquer *all* her problems if she just had the courage to try.

That Night.

It stood in capitalised italics in her memory. Her deliciously guilty secret. Her infamous one-night stand.

She had forbidden herself to think about it during the day, although there was no keeping Adam out of her night-time fantasies—which was exactly where he belonged, she told herself sternly. She had never heard another peep out of Cleo about that evening, and her chief feeling was one of ardent relief that she had got away with her reckless stunt. But one tiny, primitive part of her couldn't help harbouring a brooding disappointment that Adam obviously hadn't asked Derek for a return visit from the non-existent 'Eve'. It would almost be worth having her cover blown to have him affirm that he had enjoyed their night of unbridled passion so much that he wanted to repeat the experience.

But, given the way that she had left, sneaking out before dawn while he was still asleep, and her parting gesture, she knew she should count herself lucky that there had been no embarrassing repercussions.

'Here! Turn here! Now! Now!' A stubby freckled finger stabbed in front of her nose.

'Yes, I can see the sign,' she said mildly.

Sir Frank gave a wry chuckle as they flashed past the huge billboard advertising the Palm Cove condominium and marina development and turned off the main highway onto the wide, winding road which cut across the narrow, hilly peninsula of land jutting out into the waters of the Hauraki Gulf.

'Sorry, it's just that I'm looking forward to seeing Hazel's face when I tell her that all her worries are over.' He beamed smugly as he envisaged his sister-in-law's gratitude.

Since his doctor had diagnosed his heart condition Sir Frank had been trying to cut back on his stress levels, with mixed success. He had given up driving, fatty foods and smoking his beloved cigars, but he had found it harder to relinquish his habit of command. Selling the large development company which he had expanded from the single soft furnishings store he had inherited from his father was proving a wrench, even though it was staying more or less in the family—bought by a corporation headed by the man who was on the verge of marrying Hazel's orphaned grand-daughter.

At sixty-six, Sir Frank complained that he was too young to stagnate, but even when he had handed responsibility for Harriman Developments over to Carolyn's new husband and retired to the family property adjoining the Palm Cove marina, Regan suspected he wouldn't be idle. He would just nose around until he found something else to engage his restless energies.

'Not quite over,' Regan said. 'I don't know how much help I'm going to be—I've never organised a big wedding before.' She and Michael had been married in a register office.

He waved a dismissive hand. 'Hazel knows what has to be done; she just needs a sympathetic someone to do all the running around until she's fit on her feet again. And you're a relative—she knows you, so she can't complain I'm foisting a total stranger on her...'

'Only a very distant relative. I still think you should have warned her I was coming,' said Regan uneasily. 'She might have rather have help from someone closer in the family—'

Sir Frank shuddered. 'The *last* thing she wants is any of that bossy lot moving in for the duration—they'd try to take over and ruin it for Hazel. No children of her own left to fuss over, y'see, and Carolyn's her only grandchild, so this'll be the last wedding she gets to play an important part in...I just want to make sure she doesn't overdo it.'

Regan could feel his frown fill the car. 'At her age a sprained ankle and broken wrist are nothing to be sneezed at,' he added darkly. 'She's lucky she didn't break her neck rolling down that hill. Old ladies' bones can snap like dry twigs, you know—I asked my doctor about it.'

Browbeat it out of him, more like.

Knowing that Hazel Harriman was only two years older than Sir Frank—who would howl if anyone called him an old man—Regan bit her tongue. She suspected that the crusty bachelor carried a torch for his elder brother's widow, and by dragooning Regan into helping with the run-up to Carolyn's wedding—now a bare month away—he hoped to bask in her good graces.

'I *told* her she should use a golf cart instead of trudging up and down all those gullies,' he grumped. 'Trouble is, she's too damned thrifty to rent one, no matter that John left her as rich as Croesus! Well, I shall just have to *buy* her one myself, that's all. I could get it done up in snazzy colours…maybe with her name painted on it. D'you think she'd like that?'

Regan had only met Hazel Harriman twice, but had recognised her at first sight as a lady of countrified elegance and good breeding. 'Uh, I think something a little more discreet might be preferable, Sir Frank,' she advised.

'I know you insisted it be *Sir* Frank at head office, but you don't have to "Sir" me everywhere else, too.' He tripped off on another tangent. 'Your mother would turn in her grave to hear you calling me by a silly title…'

Regan swallowed a chuckle 'My mother's not dead,' she pointed out.

She took another well-signposted fork at the top of a hill which gave her a temporary view of both sides of the peninsula. The gentle north-facing slopes were crowded with modern houses, motels and holiday homes leading down to flat, white sandy beaches lapped by a clear blue-green sea, while on the less fashionable southerly side the housing was more old-fashioned and rocky cliffs descended to small, pebbly inlets and the deep natural harbour where fishermen and yachties moored their boats.

'Might as well be!' Sir Frank replied with his customary contempt for tact. 'Buried in that compound with all those religious loonies. Never did hold with cults. Look what they brainwashed Joanne into doing—abandoning her only child and emigrating to the middle of the Australian desert!'

'It was hardly abandonment; I *was* eighteen,' said Regan. If anything, it had been a relief to wave goodbye to her mother at the airport. Joanne Baker had grown ever more narrow-minded and unpleasant to live with in the years following her husband's death, especially when her daughter had refused to embrace her apocalyptic beliefs.

Her companion hurrumphed. 'She should have at least made sure you were settled in at university—and kept in touch.'

'She *did* write to you about me before she left,' Regan felt constrained to remind him.

At first she had been horribly embarrassed that her mother had taken advantage of such a tenuous connection. The Harrimans were only very distant cousins of her mother, and Regan had been taken aback when she had received a letter from Sir Frank expressing interest in her plans for a law degree and offering her work in Harriman Developments' legal department during the holiday breaks in her course. The job would pay for her law school costs, accommodation fees for the university hostel, and allow her to save a little.

'Good thing she did, too—because you never would have looked us up, would you? You need to be brash to get on in this world. Like that husband of yours! Michael wasn't slow about approaching me for a job—very up-front about it, he was...telling me that he wanted to be able to afford to make a good home for his wife and family.'

'Yes, I know.' Regan couldn't help the clipped tone of her voice.

She had been careful never to act like an encroaching poor relation, but soon after they'd been married Michael had announced his discontent with his real estate job and had persuaded her that it was selfish to deny him the chance to fast-track his sales career through her family contacts. So she had got him an appointment with Sir Frank and he had talked himself into a job with the marketing team being set up for the Palm Cove condominiums, at that time still in the initial planning stages.

Michael had always been very glib.

'Now, now—I didn't meant to bring up unhappy memories.' Sir Frank patted her arm vigorously, with a dangerous disregard for her steering. 'I know you're still finding it difficult to carry on without him. Maybe staying at Palm Cove for a few weeks is just the tonic you need.'

Regan managed a strained smile at his heavy-handed sympathy. His kindness made her feel guiltier than ever about her ulterior motive for agreeing to assist in his timely—for her—family crisis.

'I'm sure it will,' she muttered.

'You could have come to us after he died, you know,' he added, piling on the coals of fire. 'Hazel would have known how to look after you. She had a bad time of it herself when m'brother died!'

'I needed to know that I could make my own way,' Regan defended herself awkwardly.

'I know, I know—you're touchy about your independence. Still, I could have given you some advice about the house. It was a bad time to sell—with the market in a slump.'

Unfortunately, Regan hadn't had any choice in the matter.

'It was far too big for one person.'

Sir Frank believed she was comfortably situated financially, and she preferred to leave it that way.

'If you didn't want to stay at the house we could have put you into one of the show condos—it's only an hour's drive from Auckland; you could still have commuted to your job...'

'I might not have a job when the new boss takes over,' said Regan lightly, her fingers tightening on the wheel at the thought of the new regime that was poised to send in the auditors before the final purchase agreement was signed.

'Oh, Wade's a shrewd judge of character—he's tough, he's demanding, but he's honourable and fair—he'll look at your record and realise it's not just nepotism that got you the job!'

Regan had never heard of Carolyn's fiancé, an Auckland businessman with worldwide connections, but Sir Frank had assured her that Joshua Wade was highly respected in financial circles. 'Fred tells me you're one of the best legal aides he's ever had—meticulous to a fault! He thinks you've got big potential—'

He broke off, and Regan's knuckles whitened further as she guessed what he was thinking. Sir Frank had curbed his disappointment when she had notified him that she was dropping out, assuming that she was suffering from an understandable excess of grief and that when it passed she would regain her enthusiasm for law. In the meantime, he had had Fred Stevenson in the legal office to take her on as a full-time employee.

'He was very miffed when I said that I was going to steal you away for few weeks for a roving assignment.' Sir Frank regained his bounce. 'But I told him it was one of the privileges of rank and since I wouldn't have the rank for much longer he should cut me some slack.'

'I did offer to take part of it as my holiday entitlement—' began Regan.

'Nonsense—we can't have you paying for the privilege of helping us out!' he huffed. 'Besides, you offered to work in the Palm Cove site office in your spare time, so that'll square things up with the books.'

It was an unfortunate choice of phrase, but Regan certainly hoped so!

'Ahh, home James!'

They had reached almost to the nature reserve at the tip of promontory, the road dividing into two—one route leading to the reserve carpark, the other passing between the gates of a massive drystone wall emblazoned with the Palm Cove name and logo in solid brass, glowing in the late-afternoon sun.

'Impressive, isn't it? Michael never brought you up here, did he?'

She shook her head. 'No, although I've seen the publicity

brochures and newspaper ads.' Michael had been extremely careful to keep her well away from anything to do with his work at Palm Cove.

On the other side of the wall the rolling green fields of a massive new subdivision stretched before them. The roads which snaked through the pegged-out sites were broad and palm-lined, and the numerous houses already under construction looked hugely palatial. Beyond, marching down towards the glittering sea, were the fully completed parts of the project—the country club with its eighteen-hole golf course and the triple tower of condominiums rising from the banks of the canal that formed the man-made marina. She knew from the photos that when they got closer they would see the multi-level paved terraces that surrounded the cafés, bars and shops at the base of the towers, and, flanking the canal moorings on both sides, blocks of two-storeyed condominiums stretching right down to the sea, so that true boating fanatics could walk straight out of their expensive living rooms onto their expensive yachts.

Regan turned up the narrow private road indicated by Sir Frank, following it through the thicket of mature native bush which fringed the edge of the new subdivision, completely screening it from sight of the adjoining property. The road wound out of the trees again and a house came into view—a huge, sprawling, double-storeyed white wooden villa, a graceful old lady from a bygone era surrounded by a crinoline of verandahs and set in what seemed like acres of ground—a mixture of formal plantings and rambling natural wilderness. The back of the house had a clear view to the sea, the front was a welcoming smile of curved flowerbeds, bursting with late summer roses.

Regan drew up where directed, around the side of the house, in front of a six-door garage which looked as if it might have been converted from stables.

She stretched the kinks in her legs as she got out of the

car, glad she had worn an uncrushable camel skirt with her cool leaf-green summer blouse, but when she tried to get her bags out of the car boot, Sir Frank hustled her away.

'Beatson will get those and put the car away—Steve's our caretaker and odd-job man—chauffeur, too, if you need him.'

Regan was staring at something around the back of the house. 'Is that gazebo on an *island*?'

Sir Frank chuckled at her astounded expression. 'Hazel's idea—thought it would be a romantic place to go for al fresco lunches. Had to have a brute of bulldozers in to dig the lake and divert a stream to feed it.' His blue eyes twinkled brightly in his plump red face. 'Why don't I go and break the good news about your arrival while you take a stroll in the fresh air...?'

Since Regan would sooner not be around when Sir Frank broke his 'good news' to his sister-in-law, in case it fell badly flat, she accepted his suggestion with alacrity.

The small oval lake was a marvel of engineering, and she wandered out onto the small wooden jetty where two small rowboats were moored and looked across the narrow divide of water at the latticed gazebo, guessing that the huge spreading oak that dappled the grass on one end of the little island had been there long before the bulldozers had moved it, probably as long as the main house itself.

The hot afternoon sun beat down on her unprotected head and she was drawn across the wide, luxuriant lawn to walk in the cool shade of the wild wood which grew along one side of the house. The undergrowth to the mature canopy of deciduous and evergreen trees was a mingling of native and exotic shrubs and seedlings, and Regan idly plucked a large, glossy leaf as she turned to view the building from this new aspect.

A movement at one of the ground-floor windows caught her eye and she saw the figure of a man talking on the telephone, pacing restlessly back and forth past the open sash. She was at least a hundred metres away, and at first all she registered was that he was dressed in a suit and that he was tall and dark-haired, but then he halted by the window, glancing up from the sheaf of papers in his hand, and she got a good look at him full-face.

A thrill of dumbfounded horror turned her blood to ice.

Adam!

The leaf fluttered to the grass as her hand flew to her mouth.

He noticed her at the very instant of her appalled recognition, and for a moment they were both motionless, staring at each other.

Even at a hundred metres she could read his body language. His back stiffened in surprise and then his torso tilted forward in puzzlement. He moved right up to the open window and she began to edge backwards into the undergrowth, praying that he wouldn't realise who it was that he was seeing. Surely in her summery skirt, short-sleeved blouse and simple flat shoes she was a far cry from the sophisticated Eve whom he had tumbled in his bed.

The phone still plastered to the side of his head, he suddenly thrust his shoulders out of the window.

'Hey—you!'

Regan's body jerked. She took another step back. No—this nightmare couldn't be happening. Not here—not now!

'Hey! Don't go!' To her horror he dropped the phone from his ear and put one long leg over the windowsill. 'Eve?'

Oh, *God*!

'Eve, is that you?'

He was already out on the verandah, striding along to the wooden steps. Regan whirled around and blindly fled, crashing through the shrubbery in a desperate attempt to put as much space between them as possible before those long, powerful legs hit the grass running. Even in full busi-ness-kit, with a one hundred-metre handicap, he could probably still sprint her down on a flat track.

Fortunately she was small enough to scuttle through chinks in the tangled undergrowth that would have snagged larger bodies, but as she got deeper into the trees she could still hear him thrashing somewhere behind her, hoarsely yelling at her to stop, pausing now and then in his pursuit to gauge her direction.

When she almost ran slap-bang into the sturdy trunk of an old macrocarpa pine, top-heavy with needle-like green foliage, she let instinct take hold and shinned up the un-trimmed branches until she reached a high fork into which she could safely wedge herself, out of sight of the ground.

None too soon. She clutched at her perch, the rough bark pricking her cheek and bare forearms as she flattened her-self against the trunk, holding her breath as dried pine nee-dles crunched under the pounding feet below.

'Eve? Dammit—answer me—is that you?'

To her dismay he halted almost directly beneath her, breathing heavily. Thank God she wasn't wearing anything bright that might give her away if he thought to look up. She felt dizzy, and suddenly remembered to breathe. She didn't want to faint and flatten him with the proof of her presence.

'What the hell...!' he muttered to himself. 'Look—who-ever you are, you're not in trouble for trespassing, if that's what you're worried about!' he called, his voice rasping with controlled impatience. 'Come on out—I'm not going to hurt you...'

He fell silent until the hush of leaves stirring in the gentle seaward breeze was shattered by the muffled shrill of a cellphone. An angry curse floated up into the boughs as he ripped the phone out of the inside pocket of his buttoned jacket.

'Yes! What...? No—I put down the phone and got distracted for a moment... No, no, of course it's not—you're right; we need to get this settled now...' Her eyes hunted for the sight of him as he wheeled in a half-circle one last time and then began retracing his steps. 'Sorry...we'll pick up at the clause we left off and go through it point by point...just let me put my hands on that contract again—'

Regan remained frozen for a few minutes after she had listened to his retreat. When she was certain that his words weren't just a cunning ruse to flush her out, she uncramped her limbs and began to climb down with a great deal more care than she had tackled the ascension, thankful that her skirt was cut on an A-line rather than tight around her knees and that she had no pantyhose to snag.

She hit the ground with a groan of relief and bent to brush the bark and twigs off her clothes and legs, and straighten the seams of her skirt. She was retucking her blouse into her waistband when a prickle on the back of her neck made her swing around, her heart pattering like that of a baby bird who'd fallen out of its nest.

A thin, gangly youth, with hair the colour of used rope straggling to his shoulders and round, wire-framed glasses that accentuated the boniness of his face, stood watching her from the bushes.

Regan nervously flicked her hair behind her ears and pinned on a reassuring smile. 'Hello. Where did you come from?'

And more importantly—how long had he been there? She bit her lip. Had Adam grabbed a handy accomplice for the chase?

He didn't smile back at her, his brown eyes unnervingly intense. 'Hi.'

'Do you live here?' she asked brightly, scraping at the sticky residue of pine-sap on her reddened palms.

He pushed his hands into the pockets of his baggy khaki

shorts, hunching his thin shoulders under the plain white T-shirt. 'Nah.'

He looked at the scratches on her legs. 'What were you doing up that tree?'

Her mind went blank. 'I…thought I saw an interesting bird,' she improvised. Heavens, how low she had sunk—now she was even lying to children! Although judging from the squeak and scrape of his breaking voice he wasn't really a child any more. In his early teens, she estimated.

'What kind of bird?'

'Uh, I don't know…that's why I wanted to get a closer look.' She tried another smile.

'Didn't you know someone was calling for you?'

'No—were they?' She rounded her eyes innocently. 'I must be hard of hearing. Who was it—do you know?' she asked, hoping she might find out enough to plan herself a disaster strategy.

His light brown eyes looked innocently back. 'Big or small?'

'I beg your pardon?'

'The bird you saw, was it big or small?' he wanted to know.

'Big,' she said firmly.

'What colour was it?'

'Well…brown, I suppose.'

'Light brown or dark brown?'

'Both,' she said desperately. 'Sort of speckled.'

'Flying or perching?'

'It flew and landed in the tree, then it perched,' she said through clenched teeth.

'What colour legs did it have?'

She looked at him incredulously. 'Who do you think you are, James Bond?' she joked.

'Are you talking about the ornithologist or the spy named

after him?' he responded, and suddenly she knew that the weedy adolescent look was extremely deceptive.

She had tossed him a condescending comment, expecting its subtlety to be totally over his head, and he had fielded it with precocious dexterity. He knew very well she had been stringing him a line because he had been the one spinning it into a noose!

She folded her arms defensively across her chest. 'I'm surprised anyone of your generation knows where Ian Fleming got the idea for his character's name.'

He shifted his weight, sifting his battered sneakers amongst the fallen leaves. 'I read a lot.'

'So did I at your age, except I wasn't allowed to read Ian Fleming,' she said wryly.

'How old do you think I am?'

'Is this another guessing game?' She sighed at his steady stare. 'Fourteen,' she said, adding a year to her best estimate for the sake of his young male ego.

'Fifteen,' he corrected gloomily.

'Oh…well, what I said actually still goes,' she consoled him. 'My mother thought the Bible was the only book worth reading. Novels were a big no-no in our house.'

His thin face took on an expression of sheer horror. 'You weren't allowed to read any fiction at all?'

She shrugged. 'Not at home. I used to keep a stash in my locker at school, though.'

'But that's censorship! You should have told her that she couldn't violate your rights like that,' he said, showing he was a true child of the modern age. 'I'm allowed to read anything I like.'

'Lucky you. I guess your mother must be a real liberal, huh?'

'I don't know. Clare lives in America. My parents divorced when I was born, and I stayed with Dad.'

'Oh, I'm sorry.'

'Why?'

She was taken aback. 'Well...I'm sorry because you didn't have your mother there when you were a baby,' she said, stepping gingerly.

'Why? Don't you think that men can single-parent as well as women?'

Regan rolled her eyes. She had a feeling that this gangly youth might well best her in a debate. A question seemed to be his favourite form of reply.

'Look, I really have to go.' She couldn't believe she had stood here chatting when Adam might already be back on the prowl. She had to find out what he was doing here and whether it was going to be possible to avoid him. If he was just a visitor maybe she could keep out of the way long enough for him to think he had made a mistake...

'Sir Frank and Mrs Harriman are probably wondering where I am.' She hesitated, looking around.

'The house is back that way.' He pulled his hand from his pocket and pointed over her left shoulder.

'Thanks.' She still hesitated.

'If you turn right when you get to the bark track behind that tree big fern you'll come out of the bush by the front flower garden,' he added.

She gave him a sharp look, but his thin face was telling her nothing. If he was willing to help her, he surely couldn't be in league with Adam.

'OK—thanks again. Bye...'

'See you around,' came the laconic reply.

She paused, looking over her shoulder. 'Will you?'

'Probably.' He shrugged. 'I'm Ryan.'

She wondered what test she'd passed that he was willing to honour her with the information so far stubbornly with-held. 'I'm Regan. I'm here to help Mrs Harriman organise her granddaughter's wedding.'

Something flickered in his eyes, but he didn't respond and she offered him a cheerful wave and went on her way.

She discovered that her trust in him was justified, and five minutes later she was politely greeting Hazel Harriman in the drawing room at the front of the house and apologising for the state of her hands.

'You look as if you've been pulled through a hedge backwards, lass!' Sir Frank said, when she'd explained that she had strayed off the path amongst the trees and tripped over some creepers.

'Trust you to be blunt to the point of rudeness, Frank,' said the tall, thin, elegantly dressed woman on the Victorian sofa. Her strapped right ankle was propped on a footstool and a lightweight fibreglass cast covered her left arm from the base of her fingers to her elbow. A single crutch was propped against the arm of the sofa and an open *Brides* magazine lay on the polished mahogany occasional table beside her knee, along with the remains of her afternoon tea.

She turned a coolly gracious smile up to Regan, her dark brown eyes compassionate for her obvious embarrassment.

'Take no notice, my dear. I designed these grounds specifically to tempt people to explore rather than just to stand and stare.' She tilted her beautifully coiffured ash-blonde head. 'Won't you sit down? I'll ask Mrs Beatson to bring you a refreshing cool drink or cup of tea.'

'Tea, please,' elected Sir Frank. 'And scones. With cream and some of that homemade kiwi fruit jam of yours.'

His sister-in-law gave him a quelling look. 'Plain tea and biscuits is all you'll get from Alice,' she said firmly. 'The doctor sent her your diet sheet.'

'I think I may have ended up with some tree sap on my skirt as well,' said Regan, declining to besmirch any of the antique cream and white striped armchairs. Her nerves were on full alert as she tried to pay full attention to her hostess while also keeping one wary eye on the door for Adam, half expecting him to burst in and denounce her for a wanton harlot. 'Perhaps it would be better if I changed first...'

'Of course, and you might like a shower after your hot drive, too. Why don't I get Alice to show you to your room? Although you'll forgive us if the bed isn't made up yet, since we weren't expecting any more guests today.' She slanted a look at her brother-in-law which made him scowl sheepishly.

'I'm sorry. I quite understand, Mrs Harriman. I don't want to be a burden—I can make up the bed myself if someone shows me where the linen cupboard is,' said Regan. Whatever discussion had gone on between them before she'd arrived, it was evident that Sir Frank's steam-roller generosity had paid off, but that Hazel Harriman was gracefully making him aware of her displeasure.

The smile in the soft brown eyes shifted from one of politeness to genuine warmth. 'Now *I'm* the one embarrassing you, Regan—forgive me, but I couldn't resist that little dig at Frank. You don't have to feel awkward—I know exactly what he's like. This idea of his was probably sprung on you with much the same lack of notice as he gave me. He calls my side of the family bossy, but he really takes the cake!'

'Cake, huh!' Sir Frank rumbled. 'Tea and biscuits is all I get around here!'

'And please do call me Hazel,' the other woman went on, as if he hadn't spoken, 'because we want to be comfortable with each other if we're going to be working side by side for the next few weeks. Much as I hate to admit it, I *do* need someone to help—I'm left-handed and I have endless letters and lists still to deal with. And Carolyn is in such a mental tizzy that she can't seem to concentrate on anything at the moment...'

One of the tight knots of tension loosened in Regan's

chest at the rueful admission of relief. At least now, on top of her other worries, she needn't fear that she was leeching off a reluctant hostess.

'Now, why don't you go upstairs with Alice and settle in?' Hazel ordered briskly. 'And later she can show you around the house, so you can get your bearings. We can leave our little get-to-know-you chat until later. Meanwhile, I suppose I should see how the meal will stretch to two extra...I think Alice told me she was doing a stuffed salmon...'

Oh, God, was she going to have to face Adam across a formal table?

'You said you weren't expecting *any more* guests?' Regan blurted. 'Does that mean you have some staying here already?'

She held her breath until Hazel shook her head, her soft-set curls shimmering. 'Not staying, no—except for Carolyn, of course, and she often flits back to Auckland to stay overnight at her flat. No, by "guests" I meant that Carolyn's having a little impromptu party here later this evening for some of our local friends. It'll be a nice, informal introduction for you.

'And we do have plenty of visitors popping in and out during the course of the day. Joshua's staying down at Palm Court, and he regularly drops by to see Carolyn, and there's Christopher, of course—that's Joshua's brother.'

Thinking about it later in her room Regan, pondered the uneasy look that Hazel had exchanged with Sir Frank when she'd mentioned Christopher Wade and then hurriedly changed the subject—thwarting any further casual enquiry about male visitors. Was the fiancé's brother considered some kind of problem? Could *he* be her Adam?

If so, she didn't run into him when the stoic Alice Beatson finally winkled her out of her room for a nerve-wracking tour of the house. The room in which she had

seen him proved to be a blessedly empty library, and dinner
turned out to be a straightforward foursome with the
Harrimans. Carolyn, whom she'd never met before, seemed
perfectly pleasant when introduced, but rather disconcert-
ingly edgy when she learned the purpose for Regan's visit.
Beneath the superficial gloss of sophistication often provided by inherited wealth she seemed rather young for her
twenty-two years, and Regan had misgivings about the wil-
ful curve to her lovely mouth and the highly-strung quality
to her darting conversation. She had a beautiful figure and
long, natural blonde hair which she kept twitching over her
shoulder, and there was a hectic glitter in her golden-brown
eyes as she bubbled excitedly about Joshua, whom she
called her Darling Jay, and the people Regan was likely to
meet later that night.

A good percentage of them were male, and as Regan
ventured down later to join the party she was deeply fatal-
istic, determined that whatever happened she would brazen
things out. Now that she had calmed down she had rea-
soned that a confrontation with Adam might be highly embarrassing but it wasn't the end of the world. Plenty of
women had to endure the social awkwardness of running
into inconvenient ex-lovers. And Adam was a sophisticated
man, unlikely to want a public fuss any more than she did.

The 'little' impromptu party had the house bulging at the
seams already, and after Hazel had introduced her without
incident to several bunches of friendly, relaxed people
Regan felt confident enough to grab a glass of non-
alcoholic punch and wing it on her own. In her black flip
skirt and plain white silk camisole she knew she looked
more subdued than most of the younger women present,
and that suited her perfectly.

'Hi, sweetie—you're definitely a new face around here.'
As she moved away from the punch bowl she was accosted
by a handsome, dark-haired young man with a cocky smile

and to-die-for blue eyes who fell into step beside her. 'Now, you can't be a friend of Caro's or we would have met before—are you part of the local gentry?'

'I'm Regan Frances. I'm a house-guest here.' That was the unfussy label Hazel had used in her introductions.

'Are you indeed? Lucky thing! My name is Chris.'

She stopped by the French doors to the glass conservatory. 'Christopher Wade?'

He leaned his hand on the doorframe above her head and raised his eyebrows in a wicked leer. 'Ah, I see my fame has preceded me. What have you heard? How brilliant I am? How witty and good-looking? It's all true, I tell you!'

She laughed. 'I can see that.'

'A woman of exquisite discernment.' He grinned, and for the next few minutes elicited a string of giggles with his nonsense.

Regan was so busy enjoying the performance that she wasn't aware of her danger until a masculine arm suddenly shot into her line of vision, holding out another full glass of beverage.

'You appear to have run out of punch, *Mrs Frances*—why don't you take mine? It seems my brother is too intent on flirting to do his duty as a gentleman.'

Regan stared, not at the glass in the manicured hand, but at the stud securing the French cuff of the dazzling white sleeve—a solid gold cufflink inset with New Zealand jade. Her gaze slowly travelled up the length of the white arm to collide with a pair of murderous steel-grey eyes.

'Y-your brother?' she stuttered, not noticing the young man had stiffened at her side.

He knew her name. He must have asked about her. The cat was well and truly out of the bag.

His smile was lethally unamused. Her eyes shifted to Carolyn, clinging to his other elbow, and to the huge diamond flashing on her finger. Shock punched her in the

stomach as her brain clicked back into gear and worked
through all the clues she'd stupidly missed.

Owns a corporation—therefore must be quite a bit older
than Carolyn; well-respected in financial circles—meaning
millionaire; corporate-apartment-type rich; 'Darling Jay...'

Jay...JA...Joshua Adam.

Joshua Adam Wade.

Oh, God—she had slept with her employer's grand-
niece's fiancé! The passionate fantasy lover who had told
her he despised people who cheated on their partners was
the very man whose wedding she was here to help arrange!

CHAPTER SIX

'How long have you been engaged?' Regan croaked, sipping on her fresh glass of punch.

'Nearly two months,' preened Carolyn, looking adoringly up at the man at her side. In a pink taffeta shift overlaid with a black satin and lace Empire-line dress she looked the perfect accessory to her fiancé's monochrome white shirt and black trousers. As a woman who had never had to work—and probably never would—she had plenty of time to devote to her appearance. 'We got engaged in the second week of February, didn't we, Jay Darling? Up here—on St Valentine's Day!'

Regan choked, spluttering liquid back into her glass. That was only two days after her own encounter with 'Adam'!

'Sorry, a piece of fruit pulp must have gone down the wrong way,' she said, as Chris gave her a light tap on the back.

At least Joshua hadn't been engaged when he had 'engaged' himself to be entertained by one of Derek's 'friends'!

But he hadn't just decided he wanted to get married and hunted out a wife within the space of two days. And if he had already been involved with Carolyn why hadn't he looked to *her* to satisfy his libido instead of seeking casual sex with a stranger...or did he come from that chauvinistic school which divided the whole of womankind into only two types: those you slept with and those you married?

But, no—looking at the golden-blonde's flushed cheeks, and the way she was leaning her breasts into Joshua's side,

her eyes avidly darting between the two males, Regan got
the strong impression that in spite of her dewy, debutante
looks Carolyn was no innocent virgin. And, anyway—
Joshua was surely too intelligent to subscribe to such an
outrageous double standard!

When she dared look at his face she found that he was
staring down at her with a blistering contempt that caught
her on the raw. She squared her shoulders and lifted her
chin, proudly rejecting his disdain. Did he think she had
come here *expecting* to run into him? Her eyes were violet
pools of reflective scorn as she glared back at him. As a
betrayed wife herself, she hated that he had forced her into
a position where she felt like the iniquitous 'other woman'.

'OK now?' asked Chris, solicitously rubbing her rigid
spine.

Joshua's nostrils flared at the sight of his brother's pet-
ting hand.

'Do you usually allow yourself to be pawed by men
you've only just met, Mrs Frances?' he drawled, his joking
smile undercut by the venomous tone which suggested that
she was in the habit of allowing liberties a great deal more
obscene.

Regan's drink trembled in her hand, and even Carolyn
stopped preening long enough to look startled at his smiling
ferocity.

Chris bristled, his hand dropping to clench by his side,
as if he was contemplating planting it in Joshua's cynical
face. 'Her name is Regan.'

'I know what she calls herself.' The drawl was even
more mocking. 'Mrs Frances and I are old acquaintances.'

Now old enemies, it seemed! Regan compressed her lips,
bewildered by the depth of his anger.

'That's right,' she agreed, smiling with sweet falsity, 'but
in spite of what he seems to want you to infer, Chris, as

an "old acquaintance" *Mr Wade* knows full well that I'm not currently married—my husband died nearly a year ago.'

She was guiltily aware that it wasn't the first time today she had used her status as a widow to invite the pity she had previously always shunned.

Only one other person recognised the ploy. 'Ten months, actually, if my memory serves me correctly,' said Joshua. He looked her slowly up and down. 'From your outfit I take it that you're still not sure whether you're half in mourning or half out of it...'

Carolyn gave a high-pitched nervous giggle as Regan struggled not to throw her drink in his insulting face. His eyes glittered, and she knew he almost wanted her to do it. Didn't he care that his thinly veiled hostility was bound to raise questions about their former relationship?

'God, when did you become such an insensitive bastard!' Chris swore, his arm curving protectively around Regan's waist. 'I'd have thought you, of *all* people, would know better than to taunt anyone about the tragedy in their life.' He turned to Regan and fired out rapidly in a low voice, 'Maybe you should know that my parents—Joshua's father and stepmother—died in an arson attack on our house when Josh was seventeen. He got badly hurt saving my twin sisters and me, and then had to give up the career he'd planned to fight for custody of us kids, against our father's scavenging relatives and business partners who wanted to plunder our inheritance. I guess he feels that all that gives him the monopoly on suffering, so that he can sneer at those who can't match him for sheer angst—'

'I haven't asked you to apologise for me,' grated Joshua. 'Or speculate on my motives. You don't have to dredge up every last detail of my personal history—'

'I wasn't apologising—you can damned well do that for yourself,' Chris shot back, raking back a lock of dark-brown hair that had fallen over his forehead. 'I was just letting you see what it feels like to have someone violate your privacy in public. It's about time someone gave you a taste of your own medicine.'

Regan sensed unknown cross-currents and realised that while she might have been the catalyst for this confrontation she wasn't the sole cause.

A muscle flickered in Joshua's hard jaw. 'Back off, Chris.'

'Or what? You'll cut off my allowance? I'm not a little boy any more, to be bribed into living my life the way *you* think I should. I'm ten years older than *you* were when you took over our father's company. I'm a qualified doctor now, pal, and I earn my own damned living.'

A doctor? Somehow Regan hadn't pictured the cocky young man in his designer white suit as anything but a frivolous playboy.

Perversely, as Chris heated up Joshua cooled down, withdrawing behind a rigid barrier of self-control. 'I said, back off. This isn't the time or place.'

Chris threw his hands up, palms out, in a gesture of contemptuous surrender. 'Sure. Anything you say, *bro*. After all, you're the boss. The head of the family. The man who makes all the decisions on behalf of the rest of us—purely for our own good, of course—and takes it for granted that we'll fall in with his plans—'

'Don't, Chris!' Surprisingly it was Carolyn who put the brake on the runaway tension. Her eyes were sparkling with suspicious moisture, her lower lip trembling. 'This is supposed to be a party—I want everyone to be *happy*. Please, please don't spoil it for me...'

Very effective, thought Regan as she watched both men fold like limp handkerchiefs to dry out the little-girl tears. She wondered if Carolyn practised that look in the mirror, then told herself not to be catty.

'Maybe Regan and I will just take ourselves outside for

a stroll,' said Chris, grabbing her hand without even glancing at her for permission. 'Or maybe we'll take a row across the lake and I'll show her what the gazebo is like in the moonlight.'

Regan decided that Joshua wasn't the only one in the Wade family who took things for granted. She knew that whatever was going on, she didn't want to be involved.

She wriggled her fingers free. 'Thanks, but I get seasick in small boats.'

There was a tiny, startled silence, engulfed in the swirl of partying around them, then Joshua said smoothly, 'I'm sure the good doctor can find some medication somewhere so that you won't vomit on his romantic pretensions.'

Regan seethed. If he thought to push her into Chris's arms to neutralise the threat she clearly presented, he had another think coming!

'I prefer not to rely on chemicals to maintain my equilibrium.'

'You don't say?' His eyebrows shot up in taunting disbelief and Regan fought not to blush as she was forcibly reminded of the alcohol that had been flowing in her bloodstream the night that they had spent in bed together, making love for hours on end...

She hadn't been concerned about her equilibrium then; she had purely revelled in the explosive reaction of their mingled body chemistries. And they hadn't just made love on the bed...there had been the chair, the floor, the bath: the cold, shiny surface of the big mirror slamming against her back and buttocks, frosted by the heat from her steamy, straining body as he knelt between her legs, so that when he pulled her down to mount him she was faced with a fleeting, graphic imprint of herself fading mistily against the glass...

She lost the battle against the wave of heat that swept through her body, clenching her hands around her glass as she felt her soft nipples peak against the white silk. She just hoped anyone who noticed would put it down to the chill of the punch sliding down her throat.

'The lake's as calm as a millpond,' Chris was protesting. 'And it only takes a few minutes to get across.'

'Oh, come on, Chris, leave it alone.' Carolyn unexpectedly came to Regan's rescue. 'Can't you see she's trying to let you down politely?'

'And was succeeding, too, until you stuck your oar in,' he sniped back.

'So why aren't you taking your rejection gracefully?'

'Because maybe she was just leaving herself open to persuasion. Some women like their *men* to do the wooing.'

Carolyn stopped leaning on Joshua's arm and put her hands on her hips. 'I guess it all depends on what your definition of a *man* is. I'd say a *real* man is one who's willing to respect that a woman is capable of saying exactly what she means,' she struck back, leading Regan to revise her opinion of her as a total lightweight.

She threw back her head, her long hair shimmering like a veil over her shoulders. 'It's not as if you really wanted to row over there, anyway. You were just trying to get at Jay and me...'

Chris's handsome face darkened at her carelessly provocative stance. 'Don't presume to tell me what I was trying to do—'

'Maybe it's you two who should step outside,' murmured Joshua, but they didn't appear to hear him as they continued their crackling exchange, and he turned to Regan, effectively cutting her off from the other two.

'When Frank pointed you out from across the room and ordered Carolyn to introduce us he suggested I get to know you—since you're apparently going to be spending some of your time in the site office at Palm Cove while I'm familiarising myself with the operation there.' Regan's hands went clammy with dismay as he continued smoothly, 'So, tell me…how does a university drop-out with no qualifications keep herself such a cushy job in the legal department of a company than runs such a lean, mean operation?'

'I didn't sleep my way there, if that's what you're implying!' she flared.

'Trading favours? But you do it so well…' he taunted, lifting a hand to rub his jaw.

Regan caught her breath as the gold and jade winked mockingly in the light.

'What's the matter?' He tilted his strong wrist, looking down at it in mock surprise. 'Ahh, you're admiring my cufflinks—attractive, aren't they? And, as far as my investigations show, definitely a one-off.'

The hair rose on the back of Regan's neck. *Investigations?*

'Also unique is the fact that they were given to me by a woman,' he murmured. 'Except for my sisters, women rarely give me gifts, and never expensive jewellery. As a wealthy man it's considered my prerogative to give rather than to receive.'

Had he no shame?

'How you can have the gall to wear them around Carolyn, I don't know,' she whispered raggedly.

He shrugged, seemingly unconcerned at their proximity to his fiancée. 'But then you don't know me at all, do you? I didn't keep my family together against all the odds, and fight off the wolves that almost tore my father's corporation to pieces by being sweet-natured, mild and forgiving. As it happens, I was running late tonight and in a hurry to dress. I just scooped up the first things that came to hand…'

In spite of his logic she still didn't entirely believe him. 'You knew I might be here tonight,' she accused him.

His cynical eyes hooded. 'Let's say I thought it too much

of a coincidence that you should be sneaking around the property, spying on me, if you didn't intend to make some kind of contact.'

Shades of Ryan and his James Bond!

'I wasn't *spying* on you. I was just taking an innocent stroll in the gardens! If you think I was pleased to see you, you must be crazy!' she choked.

His mouth thinned. 'If it was so innocent why did you run? That's the second time you've disappeared on me, but now that I know who and what you are, you won't find it so easy to elude me in future. I'm sure Frank will prove even more informative if I flatter him about his charming protégée. A distant relative, I think he said...?'

'Yes, and when you marry Carolyn that means you and I will also be relations,' she pointed out with sweet relish.

But he turned even that point against her. 'You and I have already established our *relations*. You obviously think that entitles you to special consideration.'

'Do I?' Regan fenced, uncertain of his meaning.

He flicked at finger at her glass. 'You're running on empty again. Shall we revisit the bar together?' He cupped her elbow in his hand and turned his sleek head. 'Regan and I are going to get another drink. Shall I get you a glass of something, Carolyn?'

'Preferably water or punch,' Chris tacked on sharply.

Carolyn paused to give him a fierce look before she tossed Joshua a glittering smile. 'I'd rather have a glass of champagne.'

'That is *so* typical! Go ahead, then. Put your own selfish desires first, just as you always do—'

'I think you really should have something non-alcoholic,' interrupted Joshua, with a gentleness that sent tingles up and down Regan's spine. On this subject at least the two men seemed united in their opinion. She looked curiously at Carolyn, wondering if that high-strung air indicated an addictive personality.

'Oh, all right,' she was saying, with a pretty pout in his direction. 'If *you* say I should, Jay Darling...'

'No need to overdo it,' sniped Chris, and they were off again, arguing the point.

The clamp on Regan's elbow tightened and she found herself thrust reluctantly into motion.

'But I don't want anything else to drink,' she protested, dragging her steps as he manoeuvred through the crowd.

'You can keep me company.'

She tried to look back over her shoulder. 'Aren't you afraid to leave them alone together without someone to play referee—they might kill each other or something?'

A whimsical smile touched his lips. 'Or something.'

He didn't seem very worried. Stupid to think that anyone would be allowed to steal anything from *this* man.

That was why it was imperative that Regan get access to the Palm Cove advertising accounts before his auditors did. Bad enough that Michael had stolen from his employer through a fictitious printing company, but Regan had no desire to be tarred with the same dishonest brush if she was discovered trying to repay the money he had embezzled all those months ago.

She had believed Cindy when the other woman had sobbed that she hadn't known about the thefts. Cindy had willingly helped him cheat on his wife but she hadn't known—or evidently been bright enough to ask—how he had managed to finance his dual lifestyle. She had been horrified when, a few weeks ago, she had stumbled on the evidence of his activities, along with a stash of money, hidden in her garage. Afraid of the consequences to herself and her son if she went to the police, she had flung herself on the mercy of Michael's 'clever' wife, who knew the ins and outs of the law and surely wouldn't want to endure a public scandal, or condemn her husband's natural child to grow up in poverty, under the shadow of his father's crime...?

The child that should have been Regan's...

She was sick with shame at the way that Michael had abused Sir Frank's personal and professional trust. He would never have been in a position to do either if Regan hadn't introduced the two men. Sir Frank put great stock in his reputation for integrity and honest dealing, and she knew what a deleterious effect the belated discovery of embezzlement would have on his pride, not to mention his pocket, if it was uncovered by a close audit during the sale of his company. Determined that would never happen, Regan had used the information on the hidden disk to tot up the exact amount of Michael's theft and worked out a way to pay it back, hopefully without anyone ever knowing it had been gone. It had taken all the cash that Cindy had found, plus every spare cent that Regan could rake up from the sale of her former home and possessions, to get enough to square the accounts. All she needed now was the time and opportunity to put her plan into action.

'This isn't the bar!' she said, suddenly realising that Joshua had opened a door and was dragging her into an empty room.

A lamp shone on the desk, and twin pendant lights hanging from the high ceiling revealed the button-backed leather chairs and walls of bookshelves of the library.

She spun around as Joshua backed against the door, closing it with a definitive click. 'What do you think you're doing?'

'I thought you might like a little more privacy for this discussion.'

'Then you thought wrong! We have nothing more to discuss.'

'On the contrary. We have a great deal to settle.' He

folded his arms across his chest. 'First up, you can stop flirting with my brother.'

Her jaw dropped. 'I was not flirting!'

'I can read body language as well as the next man...you were leaning into him as he talked, giving him a close-up of those sultry little smiles and big violet eyes—'

'We were having a *conversation*. It was difficult to hear him over the music. Anyway, I didn't know he was your brother—'

'Ignorance is no defence in law, as you should know better than most. Stay away from Chris. Second: how much?'

'I beg your pardon?'

'How much were you going to demand from me to keep your mouth shut?'

'I don't know what you're talking about! You're being deliberately insulting—'

'And you're being deliberately obtuse. It won't work. You're a very bright lady, as Frank was at such pains to point out to me. Keen to make the most of your abilities. An eager opportunist. So...how much?'

Her slender bosom heaved. 'You think I'm here to *blackmail* you?'

His eyes flickered down to the rippling white silk and back up to her blazing eyes. 'It's a reasonable assumption. You found out who I was—who I'm engaged to—and figured that you were in a perfect position to threaten to disrupt my wedding plans unless I agreed to pay you soothing amounts of cash.'

That was the height of irony, considering what she had come up here to do, but she couldn't help the guilty blush that stained her throat and cheeks as she launched on the offensive.

'What a very active imagination you must have!' she

scoffed. 'I suppose you think that I somehow pushed Hazel down that hill in order to get myself invited up here…'

He tilted his head against the door, exposing the scars above his Nehru collar. 'You know exactly how imaginative I can be, Eve,' he drawled in a rusty voice that scratched at her frayed nerves. 'But, no, I don't think you were behind Hazel's accident. As I said, you're an opportunist—you take an existing situation and turn it to your advantage.'

'Well, I'm sorry to disappoint your paranoid fantasies, but I had no idea who you were until a few minutes ago,' she gritted. 'And now that I do know it makes not one iota of difference to me. I have no interest in you either as Adam *or* as Joshua Wade.'

To her fury, he grinned. 'You were interested in me every which way that night in the apartment…'

'I treat all my one-night stands like that!'

'That must make for an extremely exhausting social life…and an extremely expensive one.' He unfolded his arms to lightly adjust his cufflinks, one after the other, watching her pupils contract nervously. 'You left a gift on my pillow but you didn't take mine to you. Was it your intention to make me feel like a toyboy?'

She felt a wicked surge of angry satisfaction and sleeked her hair back behind her ears like a fastidious little cat. 'Oh, dear, how demeaning for you,' she sympathised.

His eyes slitted. 'Actually, I found the thought rather…stimulating.' He pushed off the door and came softly towards her. 'Didn't you like the bracelet? I know you looked at it while I was in the shower.'

If it was a guess then her expression as she backed away from him on unsteady legs would have been all he needed to confirm its accuracy. Her brief burst of triumph dwindled to renewed panic as he continued.

'Because that's my problem with all this, you see. What

you did doesn't quite jell with the image of you as a greedy, blackmailing opportunist, does it?' He prowled around the desk after her. 'You had those lovely baubles within your grasp and you deliberately let them slip through your fingers. Why, instead of waiting to accept your due reward, did you creep out and leave me to wake up alone? Apart from anything else, it's extremely bad manners.'

Regan backed into a swivel chair and nearly fell over. 'I'm sorry if I offended your sense of etiquette.'

'I don't think so. I think it was some kind of planned strategy on your part.' He steadied the swinging chair with his hands as she retreated behind it. 'After all, you didn't conjure those cufflinks out of thin air.'

'Will you stop *stalking* me?' she shrilled, almost at the end of her tether.

He was relentless. 'If you'll tell me exactly what's going on?'

'Nothing's *going on*,' she denied hectically. 'This is all just an unfortunate coincidence.' She glanced towards the door.

'Don't bother. You wouldn't make it,' he warned her.

Her hip bumped the corner of the desk and she winced, rubbing at her bruised thigh. 'How dare you harass me like this? If you don't open that door people are going to wonder what we're doing in here—'

'No one saw us come in, and given the crowd out there I doubt if we'll be missed.'

'Even by Carolyn?' She drew herself up to her full height, deciding the only remaining defence was attack. 'It's not as if you're in any position to criticise *my* motives. What about *your* behaviour? You wouldn't have any reason to fear blackmail if you didn't know you'd done something utterly reprehensible.' A mist of red covered her vision as she got to the crux of her inner anger. 'You virtually bounced out of bed with me to rush up here and propose to *her*!'

His grey eyes went dark. 'I owed Carolyn no sexual fidelity on the night that you and I slept together,' he said grimly.

'Don't play with semantics!' she cried. 'What about emotional fidelity? You must have been *intending* to ask her—'

His mouth twisted. 'Actually, no. I had not in the least thought of getting married again when I drove up here that day...'

Her feet suddenly felt nailed to the spot. 'Again? You've been married before?'

'I'm thirty-six. It would be more surprising if I *hadn't* had a previous serious relationship, wouldn't it?' he queried, taking advantage of her stunned expression to move closer.

This new facet of him threw all her previous assumptions into disarray. 'What did you do? Dump her when you discovered she'd married you purely for your money?' she said, using deliberate cruelty to distance herself from the odd feeling of melancholy that invaded her bones.

The twist of his mouth turned into a cold smile. 'Actually, yes. And it was worth every cent it took to pay her off!'

She swallowed. On top of all the other blows Chris had mentioned, Joshua had taken a king-hit to his pride—if not his heart.

'That must have been difficult for you?'

'She was the loser, not I. I was a rich man then, but I've become a lot richer in the last fifteen years.'

'But money doesn't necessarily buy you happiness,' protested Regan.

He looked at her, his eyes full of silvery satisfaction. 'What makes you think I was talking about money?'

'I—well, you're wealthy, and—I just assumed…'

Her voice tailed off and he said silkily, 'It's dangerous to make assumptions when you don't have all the facts. You seem to make a habit of it.

'The fact is that I *do* have some experience of courtship,' he said, when she failed to respond. 'And I assure you I wasn't even *close* to courting Carolyn when I took you to bed.' His tone became even silkier as he echoed her earlier thoughts. 'Or rather, when we took each other in all those assorted places…'

'Are you saying you proposed on the spur of the moment? I don't believe you!' she said coldly, trying to freeze out the hot flood of excitement his words had provoked. 'You don't strike me as a man who ever does anything on impulse.'

'I'm not—that's what makes the impulse I'm having right now all the more disturbing,' he mused darkly, making her suddenly aware that all the time they had been talking he had been drifting inexorably closer.

His brooding expression looked faintly murderous, and Regan clutched her hands to her vulnerable throat as he loomed over her. 'What impulse?'

He lifted a hand and she flinched, but all he did was stroke his finger down one dark wing of glossy hair where it swept behind her delicate ear.

'You don't really want to know.' His finger lingered in the crease just behind her naked earlobe. He seemed to have a perfect genius for homing in on the most sensitive points on her body, thought Regan shakily—ones that even she hadn't known were sensitive until he roused them to glorious life.

'Most women deck themselves in jewellery when they dress up—you don't seem to wear any…'

'I'm allergic to gold,' she said flippantly, thinking that lying was beginning to become second nature.

His eyebrows lifted over disbelieving eyes. 'As well as diamonds?' he mocked. 'You don't even wear a watch.'

'It broke— I haven't got round to replacing it yet.' Even a cheap time-piece took second place to digging herself out of a mountain of debt.

The door to the library suddenly swung open and Regan jerked guiltily away from Joshua's touch.

'Hello, what are you two doing in here?' Hazel Harriman's head ducked around the door, her innocent brown eyes travelling from one face to the other.

'Checking on the silver, Hazel?' grinned Joshua easily.

'Well, you know what Frank's like about his blessed first editions! He should have locked the door if he didn't want anyone coming in here, but he thinks that would be implying he can't trust his neighbours.' She opened the door wider and came further into the room, a picture of grace and dignity in her powder-blue chiffon and pearls, in spite of the wooden crutch propped under her right arm.

'Are you talking about the wedding? I hope you're not going to interfere as well, Joshua. I already have enough on my plate with Frank poking his nose in!'

'I wouldn't dream of it. I'm very happy to leave it all in your gracious hands,' he replied. 'Would you like to sit down and rest that leg?'

'No, thanks, I've been sitting down all night. A little exercise is good for me—whatever Frank has to say!'

Joshua smiled. 'He suggested that Regan and I get to know each other, but it turns out that we've met before...'

Hazel's eyes brightened with enquiry. 'Oh, really? Where?'

Joshua opened his mouth, and Regan didn't trust the bland look on his face. Was he about to conduct some advance damage control?

'It was only just the once—and not at all memorable,' she cut in quickly. 'Which is why Joshua's name didn't ring a bell when Sir Frank mentioned who Carolyn was going to marry.'

'Oh, well, at least you're not total strangers, so that makes everything much more cosy for all of us,' Hazel approved complacently.

'Indeed.' Joshua's blandness was even more pronounced.

'Frank is very keen for Regan to feel at home. I know he feels guilty that he didn't do more for you when Michael was killed—'

Regan was agonisingly conscious of Joshua's sharpened interest. 'Oh, really—he did *more* than enough for us when Michael was alive.'

But Hazel was unstoppable. 'It's such a tragic waste when people die with so much of life ahead of them,' she sighed.

'How long were you married?'

In front of Hazel, Regan couldn't flatly refuse to satisfy Joshua's curiosity, as he very well knew! 'Just over four years.'

'You must have married young?'

'I was twenty,' she admitted, with the thin end of her patience.

'The same age that I was when I married the first time,' he commented. 'How old was your husband?'

'Four years older than me. How old was your wife?' Regan retaliated, before realising that it was hardly a polite question to ask in front of his future mother-in-law.

'Twenty-four.' He tipped his head in acknowledgment of her slight blink of shock. 'I wonder how many other uncanny coincidences lurk in our pasts. Children?'

Her flinch was barely perceptible, except to a hawkish gaze. 'No.'

'A mutual decision?' he murmured.

'Isn't that what marriage is about?' she snapped.

Hazel's forehead wrinkled. 'I remember Michael telling

me one day when he dropped in here with Frank after showing some buyers around the site that he definitely didn't want to be tied down with children until you were both well established in your respective careers. He felt very strongly about it. And, of course, he was so very keen for you to graduate as soon as ever you could, Regan. He joked that he wanted a wife to be proud of, one that he could boast about at the country club!'

It had been no joke. Image had been everything to Michael. And the demands of her full-time study, her part-time job and the chores around the house with which he was always too busy to assist had ensured she rarely had the time to keep tabs on his whereabouts. Even though she had begun to yearn for a baby, Michael had flatly refused to even discuss it.

'And what did he envisage *you* doing while he was busy boasting about you in the bar of the country club?' asked Joshua with painfully acute perception.

'If you don't mind I'd rather not talk about it,' she said, casting a bleak look at Hazel, who instantly leapt to her aid.

'Of course you don't want to, dear,' she said, patting her hand. 'No sense in dwelling on what can't be changed. It's time to put the past behind you and think of the future. Speaking of which, Joshua—do you know where Carolyn is? I need to consult her about supper but I haven't been able to track her down—not that that's so very surprising in this crush! The naughty girl didn't tell me she'd been so casual with the invitations.'

'I believe she was with Chris, near the conservatory.'

'Oh.' Hazel's beringed fingers moved up to play restlessly with her string of pearls, her smile dimming. 'I didn't realise he was going to be here—I thought he was on duty this weekend.'

'He apparently swapped with someone else. He's staying the night with me at Palm Cove.'

'I'll go and look for Carolyn, if you like,' offered Regan, seizing on the excuse to escape her forced interrogation.

'We'll all go,' Joshua was swift to respond, and as he gently shepherded the women before him he leaned close to the back of Regan's head and whispered, 'I meant what I said: stay away from my brother; he needs no encouragement to flirt. If you do stir up any trouble, you'll have me to deal with...'

It was easier said than done. In the huge house and grounds it should have been easy to avoid someone, but Christopher Wade seemed to have developed a built-in radar that had him gravitating towards Regan with dismaying regularity—usually when Joshua and Carolyn were somewhere in the vicinity—combined with a thick-skinned good humour that refused to allow her to politely shake him off.

Later, when the guests were beginning to thin out, Regan sought her hostess out and asked if she could help with any of the clearing up before she slipped away to bed.

'Oh, heavens, no. The caterers will deal with most of the debris and Alice has an army of helpers coming in in the morning to help tidy up the house and gardens. You go off and have a good rest. And don't worry about getting up too early in the morning—we usually have breakfast at nine on a Saturday, but tomorrow I've told Alice to give us a brunch at eleven so we can all have a good lie-in.'

But when she tried to fade up the stairs Chris was there, dogging her heels.

'I'll walk you to your room.'

'I'm not likely to get lost!'

'No, but you could be waylaid by a gang of ghostly bandits. A creaking old rabbit warren like this could harbour all sorts of nefarious characters lurking amongst the shadows.'

'Yes, and I think I'm looking at one of them right now,' said Regan wryly as they walked along the hall, their foot-steps muffled on the runner which ran the length of the polished floorboards. With his white suit glowing brighter every time they passed one of the glass wall-lamps, he made a very stylish ghost.

'I'll have you know that as a doctor I have an impac— an *impeccable* character,' he enunciated carefully.

'You've also had too much to drink,' she realised, as they came to a halt beside her door.

He laid his right hand on his heart. 'Alas, it's true. I cannot tell a lie. I'm tanked to the gills.' He used his other hand to open her door with a flourish. 'Would you like me to come in and check for bogeymen under your bed?'

'I wouldn't like you to get your nice suit dirty,' she said, stepping over the threshold to switch on the light, and turn-ing with her body square in the door to prevent him fol-lowing.

'I could take it off.' He began to unbutton the jacket.

'Good*night,* Chris.'

'Yes, push off, Chris. You've gone as far as either of you intend to go,' came a midnight-dark voice from behind him. 'So cut the clowning and take a hike back down the stairs where you belong. They're serving coffee on the back terrace. You might want a cup or three.'

Chris turned with a fat chuckle. 'Well, surprise, surprise! Look who's here. Keeping tabs on me, bro?'

Joshua's gaze was steely and calm, his stance relaxed and yet also finely balanced. 'Always.'

Chris snickered, even as he obeyed the silent command. 'Night, Regan.' He gave her a sloppy salute as he turned away. ''Ware the bogeyman!'

Regan watched him go with puzzled eyes, wondering what he was so smug about, what it was he thought he had achieved. She cast a fleeting look at Joshua, not quite meeting his eyes.

'Well...goodnight.'

She closed the door in his face, but she had only a few seconds to savour her small victory before it flew open again, and Joshua strolled in with an arrogance that immediately made her vibrate with outrage.

'You could have knocked!'

'Why? We both know you wouldn't have opened it.' He walked around the room, looking at the white flounced cover on the single bed, the half-open wardrobe displaying her small collection of clothes on hangers, the array of toiletries neatly arranged on the mirrored dressing table.

'Perhaps because I didn't want to let you in,' she said with withering sarcasm, watching his profile as he picked up a paperback from beside the bed. 'Would you mind not handling my things?'

He turned the book over with careful deliberation, stroking his fingers across the covers, touching every inch of the available surface before he just as deliberately set it down, satisfied he had delivered his silent message. He would handle whatever he liked, whenever he liked...

Including her? Regan felt a quiver of guilty excitement.

'I did warn you not to flirt with Chris. It seems that you chose to deal with the consequences...'

'You also said he didn't need encouragement!' she pointed out tartly. 'I didn't invite him up here, you know—he followed me. And in spite of everything Hazel said, I'm virtually a paid employee—I can't start off my first day by insulting the brother of the groom—'

He spun around on his heel and rapped out, 'You're a little ahead of yourself. I'm not actually a bridegroom until my wedding day.'

He was playing with words again. She bravely stood her ground as he invaded her personal space. 'He was very persistent. I couldn't get rid of him without being rude. What was I supposed to do?'

'Be rude...be very, very rude...' His hand came up to cup the side of her throat, his thumb extending under the point of her chin. 'I don't like him touching you. I find I really—don't like it an extraordinary amount...'

She swallowed, feeling the pressure of the ball of his thumb against her larynx and the heavy throb of blood at her pulse-point. 'You shouldn't be here,' she murmured thickly, her voice vibrating in the cup of his palm. 'The door is open...anyone could look in.'

'We're not doing anything wrong...'

Yet.

The unspoken qualification lingered in the air.

His eyes dropped to her mouth. Her lips parted. His head sank, his breath a hot streak of sensation across her cheek.

'Say my name...'

'What?'

He inhaled the scent of her skin. 'I want to hear you say my name...'

'Joshua.' It was a mere sough of wind across her tingling lips.

His head sank further, the pressure on her throat increased and her mouth tilted up like a flower to the brilliant incandescence of the sun, and he groaned.

'Damn and blast!' His lips were hard against her forehead for a fleeting instant before his hands were gripping her shoulders, setting her firmly away. 'No! We're not going to do this.' There was a sheen of perspiration on his forehead and upper lip as he stared down into her dazed violet eyes and ground out savagely, 'You're a complication I really don't need right now!'

Stricken, she writhed out of his implacably gentle grip and lifted the shield of her pride. 'Join the club, buster!'

There was a rustle from the hallway and they looked across just in time to see Carolyn drooping wearily past.

'Carolyn?' Joshua was at the door with startling speed.

She halted, her golden eyes curiously blank, not even seeming to register that her fiancé was coming out of another woman's bedroom. 'What?'

His voice gentled to a note that caused Regan physical pain. 'Are you all right?'

'No, I'm not all right.' Her pouty mouth turned down sullenly. 'I'm tired. I'm going to bed.'

'But not all your guests have left—'

'God, you sound just like Granny!' she snapped. Then she put a hand on her flat stomach. 'I don't feel very well, OK?'

'Do you think you're going to be sick?'

'Of course I'm not going to be sick!' Two patches of pink stood out on her cheeks. 'Tomorrow, when I get up in the morning, *that's* when I'll probably be sick, and I'll feel rotten for half the day.' Her eyes glittered with tears, this time genuine, and her voice was shrill. 'Oh, God, I hate this—it's all such a ghastly mess! If there were any justice in the world *men* would have to go through this, too!'

She dashed away down the hall towards her room at the far end, and when Regan would have gone after her she found a strong arm barring her way.

'No, let her go. She'll probably throw herself on the bed, have a good cry, and feel the better for it.'

After his tender tone, it seemed awfully callous. 'But she says she doesn't feel well.' She remembered her earlier suspicions. 'Perhaps she's had too much to drink—in which case she might need someone there.'

'She's not ill and she's not drunk.'

'Not ill? But—' Suddenly it hit her, nearly knocking her to the floor. She clutched at the door handle for balance and stared up at him as her mind made the conscious leap from instinct to understanding. That Empire-line dress and the many-layered look Carolyn had worn to dinner would cover a multitude of sins!

'My God!' Her voice cracked. '*That's* why you two are in such a rush to get married! Carolyn's pregnant, isn't she? *Isn't she?*'

His face was like granite, his voice tight with the effort of control as he lowered his voice. 'Yes, she's pregnant, but Hazel doesn't know about it yet...that's the way Carolyn wants it. So, for her sake, promise me you'll keep quiet?'

'You weren't *courting* her, and you didn't owe her fidelity, but you *did* go to bed with her—unless you're going to claim it's a virgin birth! You heartless, hypocritical, lying, lascivious beast!'

This time when she slammed the door thunderously in his face it stayed shut.

CHAPTER SEVEN

AT ELEVEN o'clock the next morning it was an unpleasant surprise to walk into the dining room and find the lying, lascivious beast laughing and chatting with Hazel and Sir Frank as Alice Beatson served him up a large plate of scrambled eggs and salmon cakes.

'Good morning, Regan,' carolled Hazel from her position at the head of the long refectory table. 'Look who's dropped in for brunch!'

While Sir Frank grunted and waved his marmalade-covered knife in greeting, Joshua had risen to his feet and rounded the table to pull out the chair squarely opposite his own.

Damning his manners, Regan sat down, giving him a stiff nod.

'Thank you.' Now she would have to suffer being directly in his sight-line all through the meal. In a straw-coloured casual linen jacket over an open-necked beige shirt and trousers he looked too damnably attractive for her unsettled state of mind.

'Good morning, Regan,' he chided her softly, stooping over her shoulder in the process of pushing in her chair, his open jacket brushing the short sleeve of her cherry-red shift dress.

She clenched her teeth on a smile. 'Good morning,' she parroted. She accepted Alice's offer of freshly squeezed orange juice and a dish of sliced fresh fruit in yogurt and looked around the table.

She had been so preoccupied with her effort not to react to Joshua that she had barely registered anyone else in the room, and now she felt a shock of recognition as she stared into a pair of familiar light brown eyes, gazing at her from across the table over the top of a tall stack of buttermilk pancakes.

He smirked at her surprise. 'Hi.'

'Hello, Ryan,' she blurted. 'Were you at the party last night? I didn't see you.'

'Nah—I have exams starting on Monday, I had to swot.'

In the act of reseating himself beside the youth, Joshua snapped up his head. 'You two know each other?'

'Sort of,' hedged Regan, praying that the sly humour that had entered the young man's eyes didn't mean he was going to rat on her for the pleasure of seeing an adult squirm. Today he had his hair slicked back into a neat ponytail and was wearing a brown T-shirt that made him look even more like a beanpole.

'We ran into each other yesterday and had a bit of a chat, didn't we, Ryan?' Her eyes silently begged him to play it casual.

'So, did you see any more of those birds?' he said loudly.

Sir Frank frowned. 'There's no need to shout, lad, we're not deaf.'

'Sorry, but I thought Regan was hard of hearing.' Ryan's eyes were owlishly innocent behind his wire glasses.

The wretch! Regan gave him a speaking look which he returned with a pious grin as he stuffed another pancake in his mouth.

'Why on earth should you think that?' asked Hazel.

Ryan moved his thin shoulders up and down, pointing to his bulging cheeks to explain why he couldn't answer.

'He must have misunderstood something I said,' Regan supplied hurriedly, 'We were bird-watching, so we were whispering—'

'*Bird*-watching?' Joshua's eyebrows shot up. He looked sceptically at the young man munching innocently at his side. 'Since when have you taken up such a tame hobby, Ryan? I thought Cyberspace ruled your life. Although I suppose staring at native flora and fauna could be considered an advance on staring at a computer screen all day. At least it gets you out in the fresh air.'

'Nothing's tame to a young, enquiring mind,' Regan objected at his disparaging sarcasm. If he was going to be a father he needed to buck his ideas up. 'I think children should always be encouraged to find *everything* interesting and not be stuck with labels that inhibit them from wanting to learn…'

Ryan gulped down his pancake to protest. 'I'm not a child.'

'I was speaking generally. Whether you're five, fifteen or fifty, you're still *someone's* child,' she countered, dipping her spoon into her fruit.

'Yes, but not *a* child. A child is someone between the ages of birth and puberty,' he argued.

She recalled his water-dripping-on-stone technique of wearing her down from the previous day.

'According to the dictionary, a child is also a human offspring—' she persisted.

'But not in the *first* meaning of the word,' he interrupted stubbornly. 'I bet if you looked it up you'd find my meaning listed before yours.'

'Don't take that bet,' came Joshua's dry advice.

'I wasn't going to,' dismissed Regan. 'OK,' she told Ryan, finding it amazingly easy to sink to his level, 'you win—you're far too boringly pedantic to be a mere *child*. You have to be at least ninety before you get to drive other people crazy by arguing endlessly over such irritating trivia with such single-minded intensity.' She smiled at him sweetly. 'I guess that puts you somewhere in your *second* childhood.'

Ryan thought about that for a moment, his eyes narrowing behind the round rims of his glasses in a way that struck a faint chord of uncomfortable resonance in Regan's brain.

'You kept arguing, too…'

'That's because I was right, but I showed my maturity by letting *you* win in deference to your mental age. When *I* was a child, I was taught to respect my elders…'

She tilted up her nose at him and he grinned, attacking his pancakes again. 'You didn't *let* me win.'

'If you say so, dear,' she said, in the indulgent, forgiving tone that she knew men—both young and old—hated to hear.

Ryan opened his mouth.

'Give it up, Son. Women are genetically programmed to have the last word. They can never bear to allow a man to feel that he's won an argument.'

'But, Dad…you told me never to give up on a fight when I believe I'm in the right!'

Son? *Dad?*

Regan's spoon clattered to her plate, splattering fruitjuice and yoghurt over the pale yellow tablecloth.

'He— You— You're father and son?' she said stupidly, dabbing at the tablecloth with her napkin in order to disguise her shaking hands.

Her eyes darted from face to face, suddenly seeing the echo of the boy in the man and the foreshadowing of the man in the boy…the similar angle of their cheekbones, the narrow, intelligent temples, the strong line of their noses.

Joshua's eyes narrowed, exactly as his son's had a few moments earlier. She must have been blind not to have seen it before!

'I thought you said that you and Ryan had talked?'

'Yes, but not about *you*!' He had been the single subject she had been desperate to *avoid*.

An unholy amusement filtered across his face as enlightenment dawned. 'Let me guess…you didn't realise who he

was because you never got around to exchanging sur-
names? Seems to be a habit of yours...'

Regan seethed as he picked up his cup of black coffee
and took a leisurely sip.

'You mean it's just what happened when you and Regan
met the first time?' chuckled Hazel, who had been following the conversation with lively interest. 'A case of like
father, like son!'

Flustered violet eyes clashed with thunderstruck grey as
they shared a moment of mutual consternation. Visions of
their torrid sexual encounter danced between them.

'God, I hope not,' muttered Joshua fervently, and Regan
knew that she was going to blush as Ryan sat up in his
chair, his precocious antennae twitching at the silent inter-
action. She quickly cast around for an innocuous change of
subject.

'So...where's Chris this morning?' she asked.

Bad choice. Hazel's eyes lowered as she thoughtfully
stirred a lump of sugar into her tea and Sir Frank stared
out of the window and made a gruff remark on the blustery
day.

'Still sleeping off last night,' said Joshua. 'Why? Were
you hoping to see him?'

'No—oh, no...I just wondered, that's all.' In her haste
to disassociate herself from the question she allowed Alice
to persuade her to a salmon cake she didn't really want. 'If
he's a doctor I suppose he must work very hard...' She
trailed off, seeing that she had only compounded her error
as Joshua's expression hardened.

'Works hard and plays hard. He's not sleeping because
he's tired; he's sleeping because he behaved like a total
idiot.'

'Uncle Chris fell into the canal coming home last night,'
supplied Ryan. At least her diversion had worked on *one*
level. 'I saw him from my window, splashing and yelling.

Dad told him to stop whining for help, that he had two choices: sink or swim. So he swam to the boardwalk and Dad hauled him out.'

'Goodness!' Hazel covered her mouth, and Regan couldn't decide whether she was concealing a gasp of horror or a smile.

'Serves the young fool right!' pronounced Sir Frank.

'But he could have drowned!' Regan thought she was the only one showing any compassion. 'Particularly in his state.'

'You mean drunk,' said Joshua.

'Why didn't you help him straight away?' Regan chastised, her eyes flashing. 'Instead of standing there taunting him.'

'Because I believe in tough love,' he said laconically. 'He'd got himself into a jam and there was no reason he shouldn't at least *try* to get himself out of it. Besides...I didn't want to risk ruining my clothes,' he drawled with a baiting smile. 'I was wearing some recently acquired items of great sentimental value.'

'It was OK, really—Uncle Chris used to be a champion swimmer at his school,' offered Ryan, torn between his natural loyalty and the delightful novelty of seeing his father being sternly lectured on behaviour by a slip of a woman. 'And Dad did throw him a lifebelt from the dock.'

'How kind of you,' Regan bit out at the mocking face across the table, fuming over the veiled reference to his cufflinks. Whatever sentiments he attached to them, she knew they wouldn't be the tender ones that he was implying!

'I was aiming for his head,' he said succinctly, and suddenly she couldn't help the quiver of a smile escaping her control. She chewed it off her lips, totally bewildered by her reaction. How could he make her feel like laughing when she was so *angry* with him?

'I wonder what's keeping Carolyn? She did know you were coming, didn't she, Joshua?' interrupted Hazel, squinting at the exquisite diamond watch whose face was a trifle too dainty for her aging eyes.

'I don't think I specified an exact time. I know she was planning on going yachting with the Watsons this afternoon, but I'm afraid some work has come up...'

'On a Saturday?'

'Money never sleeps, Hazel,' Sir Frank trotted out. 'Wade can't afford to be out of touch with what the market's doing. You can use the library again if you need it, Joshua.'

'Thanks, but I have everything back on-line at the condo again—thanks to Ryan's genius for electronics. If I get time I might even call in and see how things are going in the sales office.'

Hazel was looking unimpressed. 'Oh, dear, Carolyn will be disappointed.'

'Maybe she'll change her mind about going sailing once she sees how windy it is,' said Regan. She would have thought that the last thing anyone suffering from the nausea of early pregnancy would enjoy would be a ride on a rocking boat. How far along was she? Three months? Four? Obviously not long enough for her body to have stabilised to the added flow of hormones raging through her increased volume of blood.

'No, she won't—the girl loves a good blow! Got a great pair of sea legs,' beamed Sir Frank.

'I wonder if I ought to go and wake her?' Hazel was pondering dubiously. She had quietly divulged to Regan over last evening's sherry that Carolyn had been unpredictable in her moods of late, and extremely touchy about her privacy. From which Regan had deduced that she was disappointed that her daughter's daughter, whom she had brought up from babyhood after her parents were killed in a plane crash, was not co-operating wholeheartedly on the home front.

'I suppose it's all part of her growing up and preparing to move out into her own separate life, but it makes it a bit difficult when I'm trying to work out what she wants for the wedding,' she had admitted. 'She's so inconsistent—one minute she's madly enthusiastic; the next minute she's yawning with boredom. One day she seems happy; the next everything's a tragedy. Perhaps it'll be good for her to have another young woman in the house who can relate to something of what she's going through…'

'Would you like me to nip up and see if she's up and about—and let her know that Joshua's here?' asked Regan now.

'Not if you haven't finished your own breakfast, dear,' demurred Hazel.

'But I have.' She smiled, pushing back from the table and trying not to look too eager to escape. 'I don't usually have a great appetite in the mornings—'

'You save it all up for the evenings?' murmured Joshua, rising to his feet in unison with his son as she stood up. Whatever else kind of father he was, he had made the effort to teach his offspring old-fashioned manners. The top of Ryan's dirty-blond head only reached Joshua's eyes, but he was obviously still growing, and Regan guessed that one day he would be even taller than his father. There also seemed to be a mutual respect and easy affection between them that spoke volumes about their relationship.

'Well, it was nice meeting you again, Ryan,' she said, concentrating on the safer of the two. 'Good luck with your exams.'

'Luck should have nothing to do with it,' his father answered for him. 'But don't make it sound as if you're saying goodbye, Regan. Didn't anyone tell you that the condominium I'm living in at Palm Court is the one I bought as my personal investment in the project?' He paused a moment to let her sense the axe that was hovering over her head. 'And my visit here is proving so…fruitful and enlightening…that I've decided to stay on at the condo while Frank and I sort out the fine print on our deal. I can commute down to Auckland whenever I need to touch personal base with my staff, and Ryan's school holidays start in another week, so he only has to commute daily until his exams are over, then he has two weeks of freedom.'

Weeks! Regan's face paled slightly above the cherry-red dress as fresh panic fluttered in her chest. She had thought that it was only the weekend she would have to endure. Joshua lurking around for two *days* taunting her with his veiled threats and stalking suspicions was bad enough, but now he was talking about *weeks* of having to cope with him breathing down her neck, monitoring her behaviour and possibly thwarting her attempts to put her plan into action. Not to mention arousing forbidden desires!

'Dad says I can fly down and back in the company helicopter every day,' Ryan informed her.

'Won't that be rather expensive?' she said faintly.

'Perhaps, but I can afford it,' said Joshua. 'I look after my own, and I don't consider it extravagant when you consider what I'm getting in return.'

'And what would that be?' she braved.

'Peace of mind.'

'And of course you'll be able to spend much more time with Carolyn,' chirped Hazel.

'There is that,' Joshua replied gravely.

'I'll just go and see what's keeping her,' said Regan, and fled.

I look after my own.

Regan wasn't one of his own. She was an outsider, a threat to his established order, and it seemed he was prepared to go to any lengths to neutralise her as a possible source of trouble.

There was no answer to her brisk tap on the door, but when she tentatively poked her head into the bedroom she found Carolyn lying on her back in bed, wide awake. She had propped herself up on her elbows as the door opened.

'Oh, it's you,' she said, letting herself collapse back against the heap of pillows.

'Your grandmother just wondered if you were coming down to breakfast,' said Regan, taking that as an invitation to enter. The bedroom was twice as big as her own, with a prime view over the lake from the bed itself, and furnished in feminine but unfussy style in eggshell-blue and white.

'I'm not hungry,' said Carolyn listlessly. In her white batiste nightdress with her hair in a single plait she looked girlishly young, emphasising a natural beauty that didn't depend on cosmetics. She probably never woke with sleep-creases on her face or an embarrassing crust in the corners of her eyes, thought Regan enviously.

'You should eat something. Perhaps it might make you feel better...'

'*Nothing* can make me feel better!' was the vehement declaration.

'Maybe I could slip down to the kitchen and bring you up a piece of toast, and perhaps a cup of tea—'

Carolyn looked at her suspiciously. 'Why should you?'

Regan offered her a friendly smile. 'Well, if you're feeling nauseous, it might help to settle your stomach...'

Carolyn's lightly tanned face had gone from pale and wan to glowing pink in the space of a few seconds. 'What makes you think I'm feeling sick?'

'Uh...last night—you said you might be.'

Carolyn swore: a very unattractive, unladylike phrase. 'He told you, didn't he?' She thumped an angry fist against the bedclothes. 'It was supposed to be a secret and he told *you!*'

'No—'

'Oh, don't bother to lie!' she cried shrilly. 'I saw you two huddling together. He told you! And he has the nerve to call *me* immature and vindictive! He gave away an intimate detail of my life to someone he doesn't know from *Adam!*'

Her emphasis gave Regan a nasty jolt. 'Honestly, Carolyn, he didn't give away anything—I guessed. In the circumstances…and after the way you were talking about feeling sick for half the day… I just jumped to the obvious conclusion. Joshua didn't tell me anything I hadn't already guessed.'

'Joshua?' Carolyn looked disconcerted, the flags of temper in her cheeks fading.

'Yes, who did you think I meant? I didn't think anyone else knew…'

Carolyn smoothed her manicured nails over her rumpled covers. 'No one does…that is, only Chris—'

'Oh, is he your doctor?'

'No, of course not!' Carolyn looked horrified at the idea. 'He's still doing his residency. He wants to be a cardiac surgeon.'

'Nothing as lowly as wanting to specialise in caring for the mothers of our species, huh?' joked Regan.

Carolyn's reluctant laugh was tinged with bitterness. 'You're not kidding!'

'So, is your own doctor up here or in Auckland?'

Carolyn picked at the batiste ruffle on the scooped neck of her nightgown. 'I'm not sure yet who I want to use…'

Regan was shocked. She sat down on the side of the bed. 'You mean you haven't been seeing a doctor?'

Carolyn's eyes flashed. 'There's no need to yet. I know I can't be more than three months along—'

'But you must have had a pregnancy test?'

Her lips tightened. 'The test was positive; I'm going to have a baby. There's nothing any doctor can do about *that*!'

They both knew that there was. 'So you—you never contemplated not going ahead with the baby...?'

'Of course not!' said Carolyn fiercely, her hand going to her stomach. 'Why do you think I'm in this mess? If I'd gone quietly along and got rid of it I suppose everyone would have been much happier...'

By 'everyone' Regan assumed that she meant Joshua, and by 'mess' she meant her precipitous marriage.

'I don't believe that, and I'm sure neither do you,' she said firmly. 'You only have to look at Joshua with his son to know that he doesn't think of fatherhood as a chore. He strikes me as a man who deeply values his family. How do you get on with Ryan?'

'He's OK.' Carolyn's shrug was as off-hand as her tone. 'A bit of a know-it-all sometimes, but most of the time he's pretty mature for his age. He has a genius IQ, you know— three years ahead of himself at his school, and Jay says he'll probably be going to university next year...'

'It sounds as if he'd make a pretty good big brother.'

'I guess.' Carolyn didn't sound very enthusiastic.

Regan took a deep breath. 'As long as you and Joshua love each other,' she said steadily, 'surely that's all that *really* matters...?'

Her little fishing expedition failed. Carolyn looked broodingly out of the window. 'Jay has been great,' she sighed. Her lips compressed. 'Do you know that he married his first wife because she was pregnant?'

Regan's hands clenched in the folds of her red skirt. 'No, I didn't know.'

'She did it deliberately. Chris was only ten and the twins were eleven, and she knew that Jay didn't want to get involved in any heavy relationships until they were older, so she got pregnant, knowing that his over-developed sense of responsibility wouldn't allow his baby to be born illegitimately. According to Chris she was a stupid bitch who began pushing for the kids to be sent to boarding school as soon as she got the wedding ring on her finger, and when Jay argued with her about all the money she was spending she let it slip that if he hadn't been rich she wouldn't have wanted his brat. Jay didn't say anything, but the day after Ryan was born he had Clare served with divorce papers right there in the hospital.'

'My God!' For sheer ruthlessness that took some beating. 'She must have been shattered.'

'I don't think so. Chris says she split for the States a few weeks later and never raised a squawk about custody, so I guess Jay must have bought himself out of a fight.'

It was precisely what he *had* done, on his own admission, but Regan wondered if there had not also been an element of threat involved. Even at twenty Joshua Wade would have been a formidable force, with the tragedy and hardship that had shaped and toughened his character already behind him.

'But that's nothing like your situation, is it?' she said delicately. 'I mean, it's not as if you deliberately fell pregnant…'

'No, it's not!' Carolyn looked fierce. 'It's not my fault, and I don't see why I should be expected to act as if it is!'

Regan frowned. 'You're not being coerced into anything, are you? Joshua might have had strong views on illegitimacy back when Ryan was born, but social attitudes have changed quite a bit since then. You don't *have* to get married if you don't want to. I'm sure your grandmother would understand—'

Carolyn's golden eyes flared with alarm. 'You're not going to tell her!'

'No, of course not. But I think *you* should...before the wedding.'

'I was just hoping things might all sort themselves out,' Carolyn said moodily. 'She'll be hurt when she finds out what I've done—that I might besmirch the Harriman name...'

'Rubbish!' said Regan, who already knew that Hazel wasn't a snob. 'I think in the long run she's more likely to be hurt if she thinks that you were afraid to tell her the truth. It's not your marriage, it's *your* happiness that's important to her...'

Carolyn heaved another great sigh. 'I thought you were here to help with the wedding, not to try and sabotage it!' she joked morosely.

Regan recoiled. 'I would never do that!' But she uneasily acknowledged that she wasn't exactly an objective bystander.

'No—I suppose you'd have no reason to, would you?' said Carolyn, in all innocence.

God, what if she casually mentioned this little discussion to Joshua? He was sure to believe the worst!

'I'm just pointing out that you do have options,' she said hastily, getting up from the bed. 'Whatever you decide, you're the one who has to live with the consequences, so make sure you know exactly what they are and what it is you really want.'

A surprisingly militant expression crossed Carolyn's face, replacing the wistful indecision. 'Oh, I know exactly what I want.' She sat up. 'You know, I think I feel a bit better.'

'Then maybe you'd like to come downstairs. Joshua's here with Ryan—that's why Hazel sent me to see if you were awake.'

Carolyn threw the bedclothes down the bed and got up,

stretching lethargically. 'I suppose I could. Did Chris come
with them?'

Regan told her about the canal and she laughed mali-
ciously and seemed to perk up, throwing open her huge
double closet to view the crowded contents.

'Serve him right!' she said, unconsciously echoing her
great-uncle's sentiments.

She hummed as she selected white cotton shorts and a
loose, flowing candy-striped cotton top and threw them
onto the bed.

'I'll just have a quick shower—tell Jay I'll be down in
about thirty minutes.'

Regan wondered how Joshua would feel about kicking
his heels for that long. Perhaps he was used to her blowing
hot and cold.

'I think he said something about having to do some work
today,' she felt obliged to warn her. 'I don't think he's
going to be able to go sailing...'

'Oh, well, I'll just have to find something else to do to
amuse myself, won't I?' Carolyn showed no sign of the
predicted disappointment. 'Maybe you could come over to
the marina with me later, and we could stroll around the
shops and look at the boats, maybe have a cappuccino at
one of the cafés. Joshua's got his corporate launch moored
down there, ready to take clients on junkets to next week's
regatta out in the gulf, so maybe we could stop by for a
drink on the deck...'

'Maybe...' said Regan, suddenly foreseeing the pitfalls
that could result from becoming too friendly with Carolyn.

Joshua was on his cellphone when she went back down,
and Regan was able to avoid any further barbed encounters
by allowing Hazel to bear her off to 'what I call my GHQ'
to show her the volume of work that awaited her on
Monday— 'Because you've worked hard all week and we
can't expect you to labour on weekends as well'.

'GHQ' turned out to be a large sewing room on the sunny side of the house, containing an impressive array of electronic machinery on a sewing table that Hazel sheepishly admitted she hardly ever used, a large overstuffed floral sofa and comfy chair and a vast roll-topped desk, its numerous cubbyholes crammed higgledy-piggledy with piles of letters, bills, papers, jotted lists, magazine cuttings and cards.

'It looks a lot worse than it actually is,' said Hazel, sitting down gratefully in the padded swivel chair that Regan hurriedly trundled forward and pointing to a second chair with her crutch. Regan obediently sat down and dubiously eyed what she thought looked like a bomb site as Hazel went on, 'Frank laughs at me, but I do have a system and it works very well when I have two hands to do my filing.'

She proceeded to prove it as she showed Regan how each cubbyhole pertained to one aspect of the wedding—the invitations, the gift list, the marriage celebrant and order of service, the marquee hire and catering, the wedding and bridesmaids' dresses, the flowers, the wine and the musicians, the photographer and accommodation for out-of-town guests.

Since the mid-afternoon wedding ceremony and evening reception were being held on the grounds there would be a lot of hustle and bustle around the house on the days leading up to the wedding.

Hazel showed Regan a sketch which positioned an enormous marquee by the lake. The aisle the bride would walk down was the narrow path of crushed shells leading down to the dock, flanked by hundreds of pots of standard roses, with rows of seating for the guests extending on either side. Should the May weather prove inclement, the whole area could be covered by another huge, open-sided marquee. Hazel explained that a string quartet would play the wedding music from a covered barge moored a few metres out on the lake, followed later by a disco.

'We're only inviting a couple of hundred because Carolyn wants to keep it small and reasonably intimate and informal. We did think of having the actual ceremony in the gazebo itself, but we decided that would be too much of a hassle, having to ferry so many people back and forth, especially if it rains. Whereas like this, if the weather forecast isn't good, we can make other arrangements.'

'It sounds marvellous. Especially since you've done it all in only a couple of months.' Regan picked up a piece of green parchment. 'This is your invitation list? Have you got a folder of the acceptances?'

A tiny twitch crimped Hazel's small mouth. 'Well...we haven't actually received any yet—formal ones, that is. There was a horrendous problem at the printers where we had the invitations done, I'm afraid.'

'They were late going out?'

'Actually, we haven't sent them yet,' said Hazel weakly. 'Joshua has taken the whole wretched mess in hand and we hope to have them next week.'

Regan's eyes rounded. That was a huge clunker! 'I thought invitations had to go out a couple of months before the wedding to give everyone time to reply?'

'Yes, but it can't be helped, and since the guest list is limited to mostly family and very close friends I've been able to warn most of the people we're inviting, particularly those from overseas—Chris's sisters are coming out from England with their husbands and families, you know...'

'*Chris's* sisters?'

'Did I say Chris?' Hazel patted her ash-blonde hair, looking discomfited. 'I meant to say Joshua's...although they are Chris's too, of course, all of them being from the same family. Did I mention that Ryan is going to be best man?'

'No, you didn't. I would have thought Joshua might have

asked his brother to stand up with him,' Regan couldn't resist murmuring and she watched Hazel's smooth, barely lined cheeks flush a betraying pink. 'I take it he has got *some* kind of official duty—as an usher, perhaps?' she prodded.

'I'm not sure…the groom handles all that side of things.' Hazel waved a vague hand, her eyes brightening with relief as her granddaughter flitted across the doorway and enquired if Regan was interested in going shopping now, because Joshua was offering them a lift, and to buy them lunch later in the afternoon.

'Of course she is! Off you go, Regan, now, and enjoy yourself.' Hazel's enthusiasm made it little short of an order.

'I don't like to intrude,' said Regan, frantically trying to think of a polite excuse. 'Perhaps I could just look around the shops and walk back while you go on to lunch with Joshua—'

'We wouldn't dream of abandoning you to your own devices,' purred Joshua, appearing like a dark shadow behind his golden fiancée. 'If you're going to be as intimately involved in our affairs as you obviously plan to be, the least we can do is to ensure you're kept well entertained while you're here.'

For 'well entertained' Regan mentally substituted 'well under surveillance'. Joshua Wade was letting it be known that he had no intention of letting her enjoy the freedom of Palm Cove.

From now on she would have to step extremely carefully if she wanted to escape with her honour intact!

CHAPTER EIGHT

'WHAT are you doing?'

Regan jumped, her sweaty fingers skittering over the computer keyboard.

'God, Ryan, you shouldn't sneak up on me like that. You nearly gave me a heart attack,' she said as he rolled up beside her in one of the secretarial chairs. She quickly closed the file she was working on and opened another.

Ryan raked his long hair out of his eyes. 'Sorry, did you think I was Dad?'

'Why should I?' But Regan couldn't help a quick glance around the plush, open-plan office, decorated with photographs, sketches and models of the Palm Cove development.

The sales team operated out of the ground floor of the main condominium block, and with the influx of ocean-going yachts and tourists at the marina from the previous weekend's regatta, and the continuing sweltering weather, they were working at full stretch showing potential buyers and interested parties around the development. So much so they had welcomed an extra pair of hands to help with the filing and paperwork in the afternoons.

'Because whenever you turn up here, so does he,' said Ryan. As soon as he had finished his exams, he had wasted no time inventing a job for himself—creating a Palm Cove Internet website, spending hours at the office hunched over a spare terminal, becoming something of a mascot to staff eager to curry favour with the new boss. For Regan that had meant *two* Wades she had to try to avoid, for Ryan's insatiable curiosity posed as much of a threat as that of his father.

128

The first week of her stay had been every bit as bad as she'd feared, with Joshua so attentive to his fiancée and her family that Carolyn had begun to look more highly-strung than ever. Even Hazel had got a little exasperated when he'd chosen to invade her precious GHQ. While she had welcomed his problem-solving acumen, and the news that he would arrange for the belated invitations to be urgently hand-delivered, Hazel had protested that he was showing more interest than the bride and eventually succeeded in shooing him away.

But to Regan's horror she *had* taken him up on his offer to chauffeur the women around to check the progress of the various local craftspeople who were providing the hand-made decorations for marquee and house. Carolyn's febrile restlessness meant that she had little patience with such petty errands, and usually found something more pressing to attend to in her social calendar, and Regan found that Hazel—insulated by her delight in the million and one details that divided her attention—was little protection against Joshua's overwhelming presence. Regan had to fight not only a war of words, but also against the insidious attraction that seemed to thrive and grow at every meeting, in spite of their mutual distrust.

'In fact, he seems to know where you are even when nobody else does. Freaky, huh? It's almost like he has you bugged.' Ryan jolted her out of her fretting with a grin that reminded her of the way they had first met. 'Maybe you should check out that watch he gave you.'

Regan flushed. She had been mortified at dinner the second night, when Joshua had casually produced a beautiful platinum man's Swiss watch and fastened it on her wrist over her strenuous protests.

'Don't make such a fuss—it's not as if I'm trying to seduce you with jewellery,' he had said, amusing everyone but Regan with his apparent joke. 'This is a loan, not a gift. It's an old one of mine—I just had the jeweller at Palm

Cove whip out a few links so that the band would fit a smaller wrist. Hazel is a stickler for being on time for appointments, and you won't come up to scratch if you don't carry a reliable timepiece.'

Regan had been forced to act pleased and thank him nicely.

'It's fully waterproof and shockproof, so you can safely forget you've got it on,' he'd told her. 'You can even wear it washing your hair in the shower, if you like, though perhaps you're the kind of woman who prefers to do it in the bath.'

He had stood smiling at her blandly while Regan's eyes had spat violet fire, her composure almost destroyed by the vivid mental video of Joshua as he had been *That Night*, his tapered torso slick with soapy water as he'd braced his shoulders against the curving back of the marble bath and lifted her astride him with dripping arms, bringing her hard down on his up-thrust hips, churning up the waves until a tsunami of sensation had almost drowned them both!

His eyes had flickered to the band on her wrist and she'd felt it like a mark of his possession as he goaded softly, 'How fortunate that you don't appear to be as allergic to platinum as you are to gold...'

'You've left footprints all over the place, you know.'

'What?' Regan wrenched herself from her memories to find Ryan edging closer to her terminal. 'Where?' She automatically looked down at the carpet.

'On those files you've just been altering...you're leaving a trail that any competent hacker could follow.'

'What on earth are you talking about?' she said hollowly.

'It's just a clumsy way of doing it, that's all. I mean, I think the actual *idea* is clever,' Ryan said kindly. 'You have a printing company that in the process of long, legal winding-up has discovered a breach of its former contract with Palm Cove Developments that invokes a lump-sum penalty repayment clause. It's just that if the data and dates don't match up in all those files by the time the bank cheque arrives, your tampering is going to look pretty obvious to an expert...'

Regan was speechless.

'I could do it, you know!' Ryan's eyes shone with enthusiasm. 'I could hack in and manipulate the software to completely obliterate any sign you'd been in there. Or, I could use a very specific virus that would corrupt the data if anyone tried to call up the original file on that contract—'

'*No!* Ryan—you don't know what you're *saying!*'

'Yes, I do. I've been hacking around in the system and tracking what everyone's doing for days,' he confided. 'The security here really sucks and the passwords are a joke.' He grinned at her. 'You're trying to put money back into the system, aren't you? Sort of like Robin Hood in reverse—'

'*Nothing* like Robin Hood!' Regan was horrified by his admiration. 'For goodness' sake, Ryan, what I'm doing is *dishonest!*' She bit her lip; she hadn't meant to admit anything.

'Yeah, but for a good cause—you didn't steal it, right?' he stated, with an absolute confidence that she found unbearably touching. 'You're obviously just covering for someone else. Those files you were extracting were originally created with a password held by Michael Frances—I checked. Hey, I hope you haven't forgotten there'll be back-up files somewhere, too...'

Regan propped her head on her hand and closed her eyes, appalled that her sins had found her out before she had barely even begun. 'No, I haven't forgotten—that was the first thing I did, because the back-ups are kept at the legal office, where I work. Michael was my husband,' she sighed. 'Before he died he skimmed off the money by awarding contracts for printing posters and sales brochures to a fictitious firm, while he actually had the job done at a cheaper price.'

'Cool!'

Her head jerked up. 'No, it is not cool, Ryan!' she hissed furiously, surreptitiously checking that there was no one else in the vicinity. 'It's outright theft. It's totally immoral and wrong. And what I'm doing is wrong, too. It's nothing to be proud of!'

'So why're you doing it?'

She shook her head helplessly. How could she explain the reckless anger that had driven her to act so out of character?

His bony, tanned hand slid over the top of her twisting fingers. 'Hey, look it's OK. I'm not going to squeal. I know if I help you we can make this work, with a few modifications—'

She wouldn't let herself even contemplate it. Help him cheat and lie and deceive the one he loved? The way that Michael had?

'No—I don't want you involved in any way.'

'But I already *am* involved!'

That was undeniable. Shared knowledge made them co-conspirators. 'The correct thing for you to do would be to go straight to someone of authority in the company and tell them what I've done,' she forced herself to say. 'Or at least tell your father,' she said, flinging herself on her sword.

'Tell Dad? Are you crazy! Why would I want to tell him anything? Let Dad find his own fun!'

Fun? Regan looked at him as though he was an alien being. It must be the generation gap, she thought. He might be an intellectual genius, but physically and emotionally he was still a teenager, super-charged on his surging hormones. In contrast she felt as jaded as an old hag.

'I'm glad you feel that way, Ryan, because that's exactly what I intend doing.'

Regan's jaded feeling vanished in the instant it took for the deep voice to reach down inside her chest and caress her heart into violent action. Her swivel chair was spun on its pedestal and braked to a stop with one immaculate, custom-made Italian leather shoe.

Joshua crooked his finger at her. 'Come on. It's quitting time, and you and I are going for a little ride.'

It sounded like something a Mafia Don would say to a double-crossing Capo. Just how much had he overheard?

'I— I've never had anything to do with horses,' she said, feebly resisting the inevitable. 'I wouldn't know how to ride.'

His eyelids drooped. 'Oh, I wouldn't say that. Riding a horse is just like staying on top of any other form of mount—you grip with your thighs and allow your body to follow through with the motion of your hips. I'm sure you'd be a natural...' As she crimsoned he continued smoothly, 'But actually I was talking about a boat ride.' He turned to his son. 'We're going on a short cruise out into the gulf, and, since Carolyn has frequently reminded me that Regan hasn't yet had a sail, I'm taking her with us. I presume you can amuse yourself here for another hour or so, since there seem to be a few others working late—otherwise you can use your key to the condo...'

Ryan couldn't help his eyes darting triumphantly to Regan. 'Sure!' he said, bounding to his feet.

'I'll just have a word with the office manager before we go. WadeCo has someone coming in to look at the books next week as part of the discovery process, and I just want to make sure that he's happy with the arrangements...'

As soon as Joshua was out of earshot Regan stumbled out of her chair and grabbed Ryan by the sleeve of his T-shirt. 'Promise you won't do anything stupid about my—' she dropped her voice even lower '—my *problem* while I'm gone!'

He squinted down at her anxious face, thoughtfully chewing his lip.

'I mean it, Ryan.' She made her voice as stern as possible, considering that she had nothing with which to back up her threat. 'No dumb and misguided attempts at chivalry. Promise?'

He nodded slowly, something like relief shimmering behind the glasses. 'OK, I can certainly promise that.'

She released him and smoothed his wrinkled T-shirt back into place. 'Sorry, but I don't want you getting in trouble on my account. This isn't a game, understand?'

'Sure.' He pushed his glasses up his nose. 'I understand.'

She was too busy worrying about Joshua's motives to hear the lilt of resolution in the breaking voice. 'You notice he didn't *ask* me if I wanted to go on a cruise. I wonder who else is going to be on board?' she wondered nervously. So far she had managed to keep away from the twenty-five-metre luxury motor vessel. On board, she felt Joshua would have a home territory advantage.

'Well, there'll be the crew for a start—that's at least five. It's really cool, Regan, and has a spa pool and sauna. Uncle Chris and Carolyn used to say it was better than a posh hotel and they were going to use it for their honeymoon cruise!'

Regan frowned at him. 'You mean *your father* and Carolyn—'

'No, I mean when Uncle Chris and Carolyn were like...you know—together...'

'When they were *what*?'

He blinked at her vehemence. 'Uh—didn't you know?' he said, speculation rife in his face. 'Carolyn was Uncle Chris's girlfriend for ages. They even got engaged, but a couple of months ago there was this big blow-up between them and then suddenly it was *Dad* she was marrying...'

The tense atmosphere between the brothers, Carolyn's attitude and the Harrimans' odd manner whenever Chris was mentioned—all were suddenly explained...

Regan emerged from the coolness of the office into the dazzle of the hot, late-afternoon sun in a zombie-like men-

tal fog. She trotted alongside Joshua's tall, striding figure
as they crossed the cobbled paving, weaving around the
clover-leaf arrangement of shops and cafés on the gradu-
ated series of curving terraces which descended to the edge
of the circular head of the canal. Most of the bars and cafés
had outdoor tables, shaded by umbrellas, and were doing a
good business from the tanned boaties and residents and
sunburned tourists who were starting to wind down, or up,
from their day's activities.

Joshua led Regan along the wide wooden boardwalk past
the first few berths to where the *Sara Wade* lay snoozing
at her moorings. She was sleek and white, her streamlined
cabins rising two storeys above the main deck, the roof
bristling with antennae and electronic gadgetry.

'Sara was my stepmother's name,' explained Joshua, as
he motioned her ahead of him up the short gangplank. He
had slipped off his jacket and pocketed his yellow knitted
silk tie as they walked, opening his collar and rolling up
the sleeves of his white linen shirt to look the epitome of
laid-back style.

'What about your real mother?' murmured Regan, still
grappling with the impact of Ryan's words.

'She died when I was two—of breast cancer. I don't
remember much about her. Dad married Sara when I was
five. Careful.'

Regan had tripped on a wooden slat on the gangplank.
'I don't think I'm dressed for boating,' she said, looking
down at her high-heeled sandals. The trim, lightweight tai-
lored navy suit she was wearing was also more suited to
an office than a quarter-deck. Regan hoped she wouldn't
feel out of place amongst a crowd of people in smart-but-
casual nautical gear.

'You can slip into something more comfortable on
board.' She slanted him a suspicious look over her shoulder
and he chuckled. 'We have lots of non-skid boat shoes on
board in most sizes. There's sure to be a pair to fit you.'

His manner seemed so relaxed and unthreatening now that they were on board that Regan felt even more disorientated. Where was the implacable sense of urgency that she had sensed when he had swooped down on her at the office?

A fit, grey-headed, middle-aged man dressed in white shorts and short-sleeved shirt stood stiffly at the top of the gangplank, a white yachting cap tucked under his arm.

'Welcome aboard, sir—ma'am.'

'It's all right, Grey, she's a friend, not a client—we don't have to make an impression,' said Joshua drily.

The man's shoulders relaxed and he grinned, his teeth white in his weather-beaten face as he replaced his black-brimmed cap. 'What a shame. I've been practising my snappy salute.'

'This is Regan. I believe she gets seasick in small boats,' Joshua supplied wickedly.

'Then you won't have a problem with *Sara Wade*,' Grey told her kindly. 'She's as solid as a rock.'

'Don't rocks usually sink?' said Regan.

'Not a rock with this much horsepower,' he smiled. 'This baby could raise the *Titanic*.'

'Don't get him started,' said Joshua. 'It really *is* his baby. Grey has captained her since she was commissioned. You can cast off whenever you like, Grey—we'll be down on the aft deck, but I might bring Regan up later to show her the view from the bridge.'

'Aye, aye, sir.' This time Grey did salute, a careless, irreverent flick of his brim which made Regan smile.

'Let's go the long way round, so you can see where everything is,' said Joshua, opening the door to the main cabin and discarding his jacket and tie on the nearest chair.

The polished mahogany walls, maple floors and plush white and gold furnishings of the huge lounge were sumptuous, and the dining table in the next room looked as if it would easily seat twenty under the glittering modern chandelier. The U-shaped galley further forward was bigger and better equipped than some restaurant kitchens Regan had seen. Down a companionway there were four large double cabins with *en suite* bathrooms, the main bathroom and a sauna. Distracted by the confusion in her mind and the proximity of her guide, Regan was nonetheless stunned by the opulence of the gold-plated fixtures and fittings and co-ordinated furniture and fabrics.

Beneath their feet was an almost imperceptible vibration as a powerful engine purred into life, and when she murmured something about conspicuous consumption Joshua said, 'We bought it from an American billionaire who fell on hard times. We use it mainly for corporate entertaining, here and overseas—for events like the America's Cup—or charter it to visiting business-people who don't like to stay in hotels.'

Following him back up the companionway, Regan guessed that the weekly charter fees would cost more than the average New Zealander earned in a year!

While they'd been below the boat had left the slips, and as they stepped onto the aft deck Regan could see the marina terraces recede behind a forest of masts as they cruised around the first curve in the broad canal. But it was what she *didn't* see that concerned her. 'Where are the others?'

'Others?' Joshua leaned sideways on the brass rail, plucking a pair of sunglasses from the breast pocket of his shirt and sliding them on his face.

'You said, "*We're* going on a short cruise—"'

'And so we are. Grey has had some minor adjustments done on the satellite navigation system and he just wanted to give her a brief shake-down run—'

'But you mentioned Carolyn, and I assumed...' She trailed off at his sardonic smile. He hitched up the knee of his black trousers and rested his foot on the lower rail.

'I've told you about the danger of making assumptions where I'm concerned.'

'You deliberately led me to think that you were taking a bunch of people out,' she accused huskily.

He turned aside the challenge with a lazy smile. 'You seem to be rather stressed-out lately. I thought you might appreciate the chance to get away from all the cares of the world for an hour or two.'

Since he was a major source of her stress, that seemed unlikely. 'What if I want to go back?'

'We can't ever turn back the clock...so forward seems the only logical place for us to go.' He shifted his stance, casually crossing his long legs at the ankle as he rested his elbow on the rail. 'What were you and my son talking so earnestly about when I found you?'

She stiffened. She couldn't see his eyes, but the stillness of his face suggested a penetrating watchfulness. She moved up to press her stomach against the rail, using the excuse of leaning over to study the boats they were passing to show him a delicate, unrevealing profile.

Now was her chance to do the honourable thing. To forestall any future trouble for Ryan with a full and frank confession. She would have to trust to Joshua's strong sense of justice, and the compassion she now knew he possessed, and hope that he would appreciate the honesty of her intentions...

'He has a crush on you, you know.'

Her head whipped around, as he had known it would, the glossy hair flaring out from her skull in a blue-black spray.

'Ryan? Don't be ridiculous!' spilled out of her lips.

'The more attention you pay him, the more likely he is to presume that you mean something by it,' he told her.

She lifted her chin. 'I do: it means I like him.'

'In spite of him being *my* son?' he guessed, putting a finger on her dilemma.

'He's a very nice boy,' she sniffed.

'He wouldn't thank you for calling him a boy. He's a young man, filled with a young man's passions...'

And foolish ideals.

Regan bit her lip and he turned to join her at the rail, his shoulder brushing against her navy sleeve as he bent to lean on both elbows, looking down into their lightly churning wake. 'Ryan loves complexity and finds any sort of mystery irresistible. You can't blame him for being intrigued, you're probably the most complex woman he's ever encountered. Add big violet eyes and a sleek little body to the equation and you have a perfect recipe for infatuation. He may think his intellect will protect him from emotional harm, but he doesn't realise that some emotions are not always answerable to reason...'

That was cutting too close to the bone. She looked at his bowed head, noting the way the breeze ruffled his hair, and the silky black growth on his muscled forearm. 'I really think you're overreacting—I'm just a novelty—'

'He watches you when he thinks you aren't looking...'

She tore her yearning gaze away from his averted head. 'So? You have no idea what's going on inside his brain.'

'I know how males think. And I know Ryan better than most men know their sons.'

'I just don't think he thinks about me that way,' she said feebly. 'You make it sound as if I'm some kind of *femme fatale*...'

He straightened up, removing his sunglasses, and she immediately wished he would put them back on. His eyes made her stomach lurch. Then she realised there was a physical reason for her reaction; they were moving out of the mouth of the canal into the light chop of the channel which extended from a half-melon of sandy beach—dotted with family groups taking advantage of the school holidays—to the open gulf.

'And you make it sound as if you don't believe you're

innately attractive to men. That unless you set out to entice a man he'll simply ignore your femininity. Why, I wonder?'

Regan's fingers automatically moved to twist her absent wedding ring. 'I'm not here for psychoanalysis,' she rasped.

'You sound a little dry,' he said gently. 'Would you like something to lubricate your throat while we argue the point?' He signalled to someone out of Regan's sight-line, and she completely lost her train of thought when she saw who it was bringing forward the silver tray.

'Champagne cocktail or tropical crush, Mam'selle Eve?'

She blushed furiously at the sight of his ugly face, pruned into a wrinkled smile. 'Hello, Pierre,' she said faintly, grabbing the nearest drink without caring what it contained.

'Actually, her name is Regan,' Joshua told his man, accepting a stemmed glass of straw-coloured liquid containing a hulled strawberry. 'She prefers to reserve Evangeline for those occasions when she's incognito.'

Regan jerked around to remonstrate, and fruit juice spilled out of her glass down the lapel of her jacket.

'Ah, *Mam'selle*, let me sponge that out for you before it stains.' The glass was taken out of her hand and her jacket removed and borne away into the air-conditioned depths of the vessel before she could do much more than stutter a protest.

'I think you might be safer with the champagne,' said Joshua, handing her one of the tall cocktails, his eyes flicking over the white singlet top she had worn under her navy suit.

'How did you find out my middle name?' she demanded.

Joshua toasted her with his glass. 'I asked around.'

She knew what that meant for a man of his wealth and power.

'You mean you had me investigated,' she snapped.

'Do you blame me?'

No, that was the problem. It was what she would have done were their circumstances reversed.

'I hope you got your money's worth,' she gritted.

The prow of the boat eased higher in the water as a low grumble signalled a surge of power from the throttle, and as Regan listed on the wooden decking in a belated attempt to find her sea legs Joshua reached out to steady her, his fingers firm on her waist. The breeze became a tugging wind as the vessel cut through the water with smoothly accelerating speed and the airstream flowed around the sleekly aerodynamic body to flute invisibly above the turbulent wake.

'Not yet.' His steadying hand dropped away. 'I'm only getting my reports in dribs and drabs. And it's mostly raw facts, not feelings. Care to fill in the blanks?'

He waited, and when she said nothing he continued with surgical precision.

'With such a fanatically religious mother and a passive alcoholic as a father you were bound to grow up sexually repressed and hungry for praise and affection—you must have been a sitting duck for a manipulative, smooth-talking bastard like Frances. He found out about your connection with Sir Frank and deliberately set out to recreate himself in the image of your ideal husband. But he never intended to be faithful to the image, did he?'

Regan sucked in a sharp breath. Laid out in his stark words the truth seemed even more ugly. 'You have no right—'

'I've been there myself,' he said quietly. 'I know how it feels to realise that your loyalty has been secured by a lie. You blame yourself for not seeing it from the beginning.'

'I don't want to talk about him.'

'Fine. Then let's talk about us.'

She set her untasted drink sharply down on the glass table which held the silver drinks tray. 'There is no *us*!'

He set his glass beside hers and shadowed her back to the rail. 'Tell me, why did you come to the apartment that night?'

'Why don't you ask your informant?' she said bitterly.

'What happened that night was not part of his brief,' he said with dangerous softness. 'But that could change with one phone call…'

She blanched. 'My flatmate's cousin is Cleo—she was the one who was supposed to meet you that night, but she was sick. I took her place, but I didn't tell anyone. No one knew—not even Derek.'

'That explains how, but not *why*,' he said, his eyes narrowed intently on her face. 'It's so out of character with everything else I've found out about you.'

'Maybe I was wild with grief,' she said sardonically.

But he was implacable. 'A kind of grief, perhaps. Was it anything to do with Cindy Carson visiting your flat? You never knew your husband had had a mistress, did you? Not until she confronted you.'

Regan thought that she would have preferred being interrogated about her attempt to fiddle the books to this painful emotional plunder!

'How did you feel when you found out that he had been unfaithful to you for years?' he goaded. 'How did you feel when you discovered that he had chosen to have a child with *her*, rather than you?'

The old, volcanic rage erupted through the thin crust of her self-control. 'How do you *think* I felt?' she burst out.

His eyes flamed with deep satisfaction as he taunted, 'Heartbroken?'

She tossed her head defiantly, the wind whipping the hair around her stinging cheeks. 'No—heart-*whole*! Cured of any lingering doubt that I was a fool for having loved him at all! Sick. Angry. *Furious!*

'You want to know what I was looking for that night I slept with you—I'll tell you: *Revenge!*' She gave a wild, triumphant laugh at his shaken expression. 'I did it purely for revenge, OK? To show Michael that he wasn't going to control me from the grave, to prove that I was as much a sexual being as his flashy mistress. *He* had an affair so *I* went out and had one, too!'

'You slept with me to get revenge on a dead man?'

He sounded incredulous. She hoped that knocked his male ego for a six.

'Not *you*. A *man*. Any man would have done. Being promiscuous means you're not choosy about your sex partners.'

'But you didn't get any man,' he said roughly. 'Lucky for you, you reckless little fool, you got *me*...'

She put her hands on her hips, her torso tilted aggressively forward as she snarled, '*Lucky?* I'd call it ironic that I chose to have my sexual fling with a man who was as dishonourable as my late, unlamented husband!'

The insult visibly struck him to the core. 'What in the hell do you mean by that?' he snarled back, closing the gap between them until the heat generated by their two bodies met and mingled.

She had him on the back foot; now it was her turn to shove, and shove until he tripped over his own lies. 'You seduced your brother's fiancée! Don't bother to deny it. Ryan told me that Carolyn and Chris were an item long before *you* came on the scene.'

He cursed rawly. 'Ryan might be a genius but that doesn't make him infallible.'

'You mean it isn't true? That Carolyn wasn't engaged to Chris when you slept with her and got her pregnant—?'

'Ryan couldn't have told you *that*!' he interrupted savagely.

'No, but it's so obvious when you look at the timing. This wedding should have been Chris and Carolyn's, shouldn't it?' She had noticed that some of the early quotes Hazel had stuffed in her desk dated back further than a couple of months, but had dismissed them as examples of her hopeful anticipation. '*You* must have been the reason they had their row and broke the engagement.'

'Must I? You don't think that, considering what you know of my character, you might have drawn another, less obvious conclusion—one more favourable to my honour?'

She felt the pain of his deep offence like a quiet shudder in her soul. He was truly outraged that she was calling his personal integrity into question. 'What do you mean? What other conclusion is there?'

The muscle flickered in his clenched jaw. 'Nothing. None. It doesn't matter.'

She didn't believe him. It had mattered enough to him to cause his tight-lipped control to falter. And if it mattered to *him*, of *course* it mattered to her, more than anything…

Joshua wasn't like Michael. Michael would never have rushed into a burning building to save other people's lives at a serious risk to his own. Michael had never faced up to his responsibilities—even in death he had evaded making any provision for his son's future. But Joshua behaved honourably even when it was dangerous to do so, even when it was difficult, or interfered with his own pleasures.

As the boat creamed over the glittering open sea, a clear shaft of light seemed to shine down from the blue vault of heaven and illuminate the answer in her heart.

But how to break down that wall of steely self-control and make him admit it?

'So…if you weren't sleeping with Carolyn *before* the big fight, then it must have happened after. After her horrible row with Chris she came running to his big brother for comfort, and instead you took ruthless advantage of her vulnerability—is that the scenario you expect me to believe?'

He picked up his glass again and took a long swallow. 'I don't expect anything of you.'

Now he was lying!

'Is it your baby—or Chris's? Or are the dates that you both slept with her so entwined that neither of you know *which* one of you is the father?'

His head jerked back at her slicing scorn. 'It's a Wade. That's all that's important.'

'And you don't mind marrying your brother's discards?'

He finished the drink, his knuckles white around the glass. 'Leave it, Regan.'

She was beginning to get an even stronger inkling of the way his mind worked. 'What's the matter? Don't you like it when the tables are turned and *I'm* the one asking all the intrusive questions?' she said recklessly. 'Maybe you three had a slightly incestuous *ménage à trois* going...does it turn you on to share a woman in bed with your brother?'

'Be very—very, careful what you say next,' he said thickly. 'In fact, it would be an extremely good idea if you shut up altogether!'

Adrenaline raced through her veins. 'Or what? You'll throw me to the sharks? What price your honour then? Oh, I forgot...you don't *have* any! So maybe Carolyn wasn't a willing party in this fascinating scenario of yours at all. Maybe it wasn't seduction on your part, but *rape*—'

'I've never even *touched* her—!' he roared, and broke off, his eyes blazing with silver wrath.

'But you're going to marry her all the same.' She was breathless in horrified awe. 'You're going to marry a woman you don't love, and who doesn't love you, in order to give your brother's baby the family name, because for some reason he's baulking at marriage and unplanned fatherhood. What you can't force *him* to do you're going to do yourself. My God, that's positively Gothic! Don't you think that's carrying your sense of honour to a ridiculous extreme—?'

She squeaked as she was snatched off her feet, dangling by her upper arms between two iron fists.

'I told you to shut up!'

'But you didn't tell me what would happen if I didn't,' she said breathlessly, pushing her hands against his chest and pointing her sandalled toes in a vain attempt to touch the deck.

He began to slowly lower her towards him, the muscles in his neck and shoulders bulging with the effort. 'It wouldn't have mattered if I had. You *wanted* me to lose control. I would have taken apart a man for saying those things—'

'But I'm a woman.' The smouldering acknowledgement flared in his eyes and her voice went abruptly and embarrassingly husky. 'B-besides, violence never really solves anything—'

'The hell it doesn't,' he growled, and kissed her—a hot, savage clash of mouths that made her go up in flames as he hooked his arm under her knees and swung her up into his arms, carrying her from the bright sunlight through the cool luxury of the lounge and down the narrow companionway into the dim depths of his cabin.

'You said we weren't going to do this,' she gasped, kicking off her shoes as he set her lightly on her feet and peeled his still buttoned shirt over his head.

He cupped her face, and drew her mouth under his.

'God forgive me, I lied...'

CHAPTER NINE

REGAN smoothed her trembling hands over his bare chest, skimming her palms over his rippling shoulders and down across the silky pelt of hair to the ridged muscles of his abdomen, thrilling to her rediscovery of his masculine beauty.

Joshua broke his mouth from hers and threw his head back, closing his eyes as he licensed her hands to rove caressingly against his skin, offering himself up like a sacrificial victim to the spearing pleasure of her touch.

'You remembered how much I liked that...' he groaned as her fingertips slid through the tangle of curls and nudged against the flat discs of his nipples. 'Yes...do that again...' His muscles contracted and his chest rose, pushing against her exploring fingers as she obeyed. He shuddered, his nostrils flaring at the scent of his own arousal. 'God, what you do to me...'

She could see it in the taut planes of his face, hear it in the harsh sound of his indrawn breath and feel it in the electric tension of his body, and it excited her unbearably to know that he was so violently responsive to her touch that even the lightest stroke could make his desire strain savagely on the leash. It had been the same that night in the apartment...his hunger for her so wonderfully intense that she had felt like the most beautiful and alluring woman in the world...the *only* woman who existed for him, the focus of all his dreams and the answer to all his desires.

He opened his eyes and smiled slowly at the sight of her flushed face, parted lips and smugly sensuous eyes.

'Little tyrant, you like having me at your mercy, don't

you?' he accused, but his deep tone was one of smoky approval. His hands stroked up her arms and spread around her back, massaging the soft cotton fabric of her top against her slender form. 'You like knowing that you have the power to drive me beyond the bounds of common sense, of decency...'

In a twisted way she did. It satisfied a deep-seated need in her to be the primal source of his actions.

'*I'm* the one who should be begging for mercy,' she said, drawing her nails delicately across his chest. 'I'm the one who was kidnapped by a pirate. Swept off my feet and carried down to the bowels of his ship—'

'—to be ravished from head to toe...' He cupped the side of her face with a scarred hand, his eyes darkening. 'But not entirely against your will...'

The taunting accusation of rape had wounded him, even if he had swiftly realised that it had merely been intended to goad him into revealing the truth. She turned her head, pressing her lips to the crease of his strong life line. 'Not at all against my will...'

Her husky confession made him shudder.

'I don't want to hurt you—' The tormented admission was dragged from him reluctantly, a concession to the impossible situation that existed outside the universe of the closed cabin. 'I've made a promise that I won't—*can't*—go back on...too much is at stake...'

She couldn't tell him that it was too late, that the hurt was already stored up in her heart against the day that she would no longer have any place in his life. She couldn't lay that burden on him, on top of the ones that he already bore on his broad shoulders. They both knew that what they were doing was wrong, but not as wrong as it would be tomorrow—or in a month's time, if and when he married Carolyn. Despicable as it might be, Regan wanted to snatch one more precious memory for herself before her conscience forever denied her the expression of her forbidden love.

It had taken months for her to be wooed around to the idea that she was in love with Michael, but with Joshua there had been no gradual awakening; the knowledge had come like a thunderbolt out of a clear blue sky—a violent, concussive shock exploding in her consciousness and accompanied by a strong whiff of sulphur. She hadn't been looking for love—quite the reverse—but it had stormed into her wary heart with a vengeance, and she found she could no more control the unruly emotion than she could the stars in their courses.

But, unlike her first, naive foray into love, this time the portents for a relationship were quite clearly disastrous, and she was prepared for the worst.

'I know...' she whispered reassuringly, loving him for his warning. 'I know you won't hurt me,' she added, her hands moving to his belt to unthread the buckle, 'because I already know what kind of lover you are...strong and virile, and incredibly generous.'

Her fingers went to his zip and he caught her wrists, using them to pull her up against him. His mouth came down on hers and he ravaged it with a forceful passion that triggered a gush of moist heat between her thighs. He angled his head, licking and nibbling at the soft, inner tissue of her mouth, drawing her tongue into his mouth and tugging on it with a rhythmic, erotic suction that made her yearn for an even more intimate intrusion into her moist interior.

His hands fisted in the thin, white cotton of her top, drawing the stretchy fabric tight across her breasts as he lifted his head to study the effect.

'I like knowing that you don't wear a bra,' he said thickly. 'The other night at the party I imagined I could see the shadow of your nipples against the white silk. I knew they'd be as dark as ripe cherries because they were so pointed and hard.'

'That was because of you,' she whispered, arching her back and tilting her head to give him a better view. 'Because your eyes on me made me want you, even though I pretended not to notice…'

He smoothed a hand across the small mounds, cupping and shaping them. 'They're hard now, too.' He found one stiff nub and fondled it gently, then more roughly as he watched her face register the sharp thrill, her eyelids sinking, her cheeks flushing, her damp mouth quivering in inarticulate pleasure.

One hand wrapped around her arched back and she clutched at his shoulders as he pushed the hem of the top up over her collarbone, framing her breasts for his admiration.

'Look, they're blushing…' he said, drawing a finger up one hot, swollen rise, tracing the blue veins that showed through the tight, translucent skin.

'I'm not surprised,' whispered Regan shakily. 'If you knew what I was thinking you'd be blushing, too…'

'What are you thinking about…this?' He replaced his finger with his hot, wet mouth, painting the entire surface of her breasts with slow, rasping strokes of his tongue, gradually narrowing his concentration to the glistening nipples. 'I remember how much you loved me doing this,' he said, his voice a whisper of sound against her creamy flesh, 'how you demanded I do it over and over again… I remember how I gave you an orgasm just by pushing my thigh tight between your legs while I sucked on your dainty nipples.'

And she remembered how he had used words as cleverly as he had used his mouth and his hands. Her knees melted, and on the way down he pulled the top over her head and threw it on top of his shirt, supporting her from hand to hand as he efficiently dealt with her trim skirt.

She was embarrassed at the plainness of her unadorned white panties, but he smiled as he hooked his fingers into the elastic.

'Prim little cottontail,' he teased as he stripped them down her thighs. 'Don't you know how erotic the contrast is between these and your own natural G-string of sexy black lace?' And he ruffled his fingers teasingly in the soft triangle of dark fur that the panties had concealed.

The throb of the boat's engine beneath her feet seemed to echo the thrumming of her heart as Joshua threw off the rest of his clothes with an enchanting, almost boyish eagerness. But there was nothing boyish about him when he pulled her back into his arms.

The wide double bunk was built into one corner of the cabin on a pedestal of drawers, its smooth, satiny, dark blue cover glowing under the strip of lights concealed in the bottom row of bookshelves on the wall above the bed, but when Joshua sat down on the edge and tried to draw her down on top of him, Regan resisted.

She sank to her knees between his legs, onto the thick, soft carpet, running her hands up the strong column of his thighs, gliding her thumbs into the sensitive patches of hairless skin on either side of his groin.

When she bent her head, he stilled, his hands cupping her shoulders. 'Regan—'

Her eyes lifted to his. 'I want to make love to you.' And, as his gaze moved hungrily down over her nude, submissive pose she reminded him huskily, 'The way you did to me...'

His nostrils flared as she closed her mouth over him and proceeded to pleasure him to the brink of madness with her soft tongue and throaty little sounds of seductive enjoyment. His back stiffened, the tendons in his neck cording

as he arched his throat and gritted his teeth, fighting the
approaching explosion in order to increase the deliciously
excruciating torment of unsatisfied desire. He plunged his
hands into her hair, guiding her beautifully eager mouth,
and when he could bear it no more his iron muscles knotted
and convulsed, and a harsh, guttural cry of groaning com-
pletion was torn from his heaving chest.

Only then did she allow him to pull her beside him on
the rumpled cover and cuddle her up to his naked length.

'*You're* the incredibly generous lover…' he murmured,
propping himself up on one elbow so that he might gauge
her reaction to his languorous caresses. 'For all you know
you might have just ruined your chances of being thoroughly bedded…'

She gave a small gurgle of sultry delight. 'I doubt it, if
your previous performances are anything to go by…' Her
breath ended on a little hiccup as his touch feathered dangerously low on her concave belly.

'Your husband didn't satisfy you in bed, did he?' He
traced his way back up to her aroused breasts and bent over
to softly moisten a rosy nipple.

She shivered. 'I thought he did…' she said huskily,
'…until you… Then I knew. With him it never felt— I
didn't— I never…'

His eyes were moon-silver as he combed her hair across
the pillow. 'You never had an orgasm…' She blushed at
his tone of gloating satisfaction and his soft laugh was
tinged with triumphant pride. 'You were so delightfully
frantic that first time—as if you didn't quite realise what
was happening to you—but afterwards you were wildly un-
inhibited, and so eager to experiment I could hardly fail to
oblige…'

He nuzzled at her mouth, deliberately abrading her
cheeks with his soft whiskers, kissing her, stroking her until
she was moving ceaselessly, restlessly, rubbing herself

against him, becoming increasingly excited as she felt him hardening against her belly, and then he was reaching for her, rolling her under him.

'Miracle-worker...' he growled sexily as he pushed her thighs apart, settling himself firmly against the juncture of her body.

She felt the blunt force of him testing her readiness and suddenly stiffened. 'Are you—? Joshua, you're not wearing any protection—'

He froze and looked down at himself, stunned, then into the yearning violet eyes that were suddenly drenched with unexpressed sorrow.

'It isn't safe,' she told him shakily. 'I haven't used the pill since Michael died. He—he never wanted me to have his baby,' she whispered. She couldn't stop the words spilling out: how Cindy had confessed that Michael had thought her too brash, too poorly educated, too overtly sexy with her bleached hair and big breasts, to be groomed into a proper corporate wife, whereas Regan had been tailor-made for his ambitions. How, to please Michael, Regan had continued with her law studies, even when she'd realised she wasn't cut out to be a lawyer; how she'd increased the hours of her part-time job in order to help them afford the big, up-market house in a swanky suburb that he had insisted was essential to his image; how she had acted as his hostess whenever he'd wanted to show off his stable home life, and nobly respected his long hours of work and frequent absences from home.

'But whatever I did to please him, it never seemed to be enough. And I couldn't even make him want our child,' she said bleakly. 'He let *her* get pregnant, but he stood over *me* every morning until I'd taken my pill, to make sure I couldn't conceive...'

'Ah, Regan...' He drank from her trembling lips and rolled his forehead against hers. 'He was a worthless cheat.

Controlling your fertility was just another way for him to
exert his domination over a wife whom he knew was his
moral and intellectual superior. Don't be sad—be glad that
your babies won't carry his genes.' He shaped her breast
and stroked the tender peak. 'One day you'll suckle a baby
at your breast, and I know you'll make a wonderful
mother...'

But not with him...

He rolled off the bed and was back again before she
could recover from his shattering words, donning the protection with deft movements that ensured she had little time
to think before he was gathering her up again and moving
smoothly between her thighs.

Sensing that only passion could banish her lingering *tris-
tess*, he braced himself over her on locked arms and
plunged inside her, each powerful, explosive thrust of his
thighs and buttocks forcing her further up the bed. His pace
didn't falter, the added tension in her tautly straining torso
and her spreadeagled limbs exciting him to even more reckless heights. In the air-conditioned coolness the sweat
glinted on his chest, forming droplets that pearled in the
thick mat of hair and trickled down his rippling belly to
add to the steamy moisture that slicked their thighs where
their bodies met.

His face was hard and glazed, his eyes locked with hers,
all his attention focused on her approaching climax as she
jerked and shuddered under his rampant assault, uttering
heated little whimpers and moans of encouragement that
fed his lust to see her come totally apart before his own
orgasm destroyed the last of his control.

Regan's vision began to fade around the edges, her mind
disengaging as her senses drastically overloaded, unable to
process the escalating bombardment of pleasure. Her eyes
purpled as she rushed towards the abyss of ecstasy, exulting
in Joshua's fiercely unrelenting possession, thrilling to the

intrusion of his hard body, the hugeness of him filling her, loving her to the hilt, and the incredible feeling of swelling tightness that grew and grew until it exploded and she screamed with the agony of blissful release.

Then Joshua was wrenching and groaning and pouring himself into her, and their bodies eased into the sweet aftermath of mutual fulfilment that to Regan felt like the settling of her soul, like coming home...

She rolled over onto her side at the edge of the bed, facing away from him, trying to control the unruly emotions that threatened to spill out of her mouth. She stared, dry-eyed, across the cabin, trying to close herself off from the press of feelings, reaching inwards for the courage to accept what she couldn't change. Joshua wouldn't want tears and tantrums—he probably got enough of those from Carolyn. He would want her to be cool and sophisticated. He might even, God forbid, want them to remain *friends*...

'I'm sorry...' She heard the bittersweet remorse in his voice as she felt a finger slowly trace the bony centre line of her back from her nape to the hollow at the base of her spine.

'*I'm* not!' She widened her eyes fiercely, refusing to regret a moment of her glorious physical outpouring of love.

'No, not for what we've just done...' His finger stroked up again. 'But for the fact that I can't offer you any more than this...' She felt his lips against the wing of her shoulderblade. 'If I were a different sort of man and you were a different sort of woman we could remain lovers, but we both have too much pride and self-respect to sacrifice honour to a self-serving lie...'

She remembered that he had quoted her Shakespeare about her being a pearl, and now another quotation floated into her mind that summed up her understanding of Joshua Wade... *'Mine honour is my life; both grow in one; Take honour from me, and my life is done.'* She could not love him half so much if he were not a man of such unflinching principle.

'I know…'

She felt his hand spread out across her back as the breath came sighing from her lungs. 'Chris wanted a long engagement…he didn't want to lose Carolyn, but she refused to move in with him and he didn't feel quite ready for marriage. When she broke the news that she was pregnant they had a fight in which he accused her of trying to trap him and she accused him of wanting her to have an abortion. They both said some ugly things that neither seem willing to overlook—'

'You don't have to tell me this—' she began painfully, but he firmly overrode her.

'That morning after you left the apartment, Carolyn phoned me from here in hysterics, begging me to come up and help. She and Chris had been rowing for a week, and she was at the end of her tether. She isn't cut out to be a single mother; she's tough in some ways but emotionally fragile in others. She had given herself to my brother in good faith and he had turned his back on her when she most needed his support. I promised her that she wouldn't have to go through this on her own and I have to stand by that promise. I owe that to her—and to Frank and Hazel, for the way that they'd welcomed Chris into their home.

'Whatever her feelings for Chris, we agreed that if we married, then for the baby's sake it has to be a *real* marriage…not simply a temporary sham for the sake of convention. I'll be a faithful, protective husband and do my utmost to ensure that she's a contented wife. And the baby will grow up as Ryan's brother or sister.'

How noble of him. The acid words burned on the tip of her tongue as envy challenged her good intentions at the thought of another woman as the sole object of his cherishing. And yet it was balm to her heart to believe that the reason he had never tried to contact her again after their original tumble between the sheets might not have been because he hadn't been interested, but because his orderly world had suddenly exploded in emotional chaos and his strong sense of honour had relegated all women but Carolyn firmly into the past.

Only, where Regan was concerned, his past had come back to tempt him to dishonour...

She stiffened as there was a light tap of the door.

'Ahem...*monsieur*? *Excusez-moi*, but I thought you'd like to know that we've arrived back at the moorings. The captain is just backing into the slips...and your brother is waiting on the dock.'

'Chris?' Joshua swore in a low voice while Regan automatically yanked the edge of the satin cover over her nakedness. 'What in the hell is he doing here?' He lifted his voice. 'Thanks, Pierre—I'll be right up. Tell Grey not to lower the gangplank until he sees me on deck.'

He climbed lithely over Regan's prone body and began pulling on his discarded clothes.

'No—you stay here,' he commanded as she made a move to do the same, checking himself in the full-length mirror on the *en suite* bathroom door, raking his hair back with his fingers before buttoning the open collar of his shirt to hide the tell-tale red mark glowing on the skin on the unblemished side of his throat. 'He probably only wants to ask if he can stay the weekend in the condo. I'll be back as soon as I get rid of him.' He swooped and sealed his hastily made promise with a brief kiss on her dismayed mouth.

As soon as the door closed behind him Regan scrambled out of the bed and darted across to bolt the door. She picked up her clothes and shook them out. The skirt was a bit crumpled, but luckily the creases wouldn't show up on the dark fabric, and her cotton-knit top was uncrushable. She

158 THE REVENGE AFFAIR

would have liked to have a shower, but didn't know whether the sound of the pipes would be audible above deck and instead contented herself with a quick sponge-down in the bathroom before hurriedly dressing.

She dashed warm water in her face from the marble basin and used a comb from the vanity to return her hair to silky smoothness. Her face looked naked without make-up, her lips pouty and swollen, and she could see whisker burns on her chin and throat. To her horror she remembered that she had put her handbag down somewhere in the lounge, when Joshua had been showing her around. Unfortunately the drawers in the vanity yielded strictly masculine toiletries, and without recourse to make-up she had to satisfy herself with a pat of male moisturiser and a dab of cologne.

Although the boat no longer felt as if it was moving, the engine still continued to hum, and even straining her ears she could detect no sound from above. The luxury interior fittings obviously included soundproofing.

However, for added safety, she closed the bathroom door and perched on the closed toilet seat to await her rescue. When fifteen minutes had passed by the tick of the excruciatingly accurate platinum watch on her wrist she paced back out into the cabin and peered out of the porthole, but all she could see was the stylish super-yacht parked in the next slip.

After twenty-five minutes she could bear it no longer. Perhaps Joshua had taken Chris across the boardwalk to his condominium. All the two-storeyed condominiums that edged the dock had electronically coded security gates that opened from the boardwalk into private courtyards, and it might be possible for her to slip off the boat without being seen, unless the two men were standing at one of the huge picture windows overlooking the canal.

She silently cracked open the cabin door and peeped down the empty corridor towards the companionway.

Everything was quiet. She decided that she would creep as far as the stairs and see if she could hear any conversation from the lounge. Her hand had just touched the smooth, polished stair-rail when there was a slight sound behind her.

'Looking for this?'

She spun around, hoping that Pierre had tidied up his accent.

Christopher Wade stood in the open doorway of one of the end cabins, her navy jacket dangling from a coat hanger on his finger.

He was looking very casual in white jeans and a striped T-shirt, and behind him an open suitcase lay on the three-quarter bed. Regan realised that whatever had brought him back to Palm Cove for the second consecutive weekend, he hadn't arrived expecting big brother to give him house-room. In view of the tension between them he had evidently chosen to stay on the boat.

'Yes, I was, thank you,' she said, hoping her voice didn't sound as nervously shrill to him as it did to her own ears. 'I spilled a drink on myself and Pierre was cleaning it for me.'

'He left it hanging on the shower door of the main bathroom. I found it when I went in to recharge my razor.' His gaze went from her slender figure to the cabin door she had foolishly left ajar. 'I knew it couldn't be Carolyn's—she never wears navy.'

She sustained his steady blue gaze with extreme difficulty as he slipped the jacket off the hanger and held it out to her. 'It seems to be cured of whatever befell it—do you want to put it back on?'

She cleared her throat. 'No, thanks—I'll just carry it; it's a bit warm.' She smiled as she took it from him, but his expression was uncharacteristically cool.

'You're going to have a fairly tender bruise there to-morrow,' he said quietly, and touched the soft skin at the outermost swell of her breast, where it was exposed by the cut-away armhole of her top. 'In fact, you're going to have quite a few by the looks of it,' he continued, his eyes moving over her bare throat and shoulders. 'And here I always thought Josh's bark was worse than his bite...'

Regan fell back a step, clutching her jacket to her chest, feeling worse than naked, her cheeks stinging hot.

'I— I—'

'I wondered why he seemed so unusually twitchy when I wanted to come down and settle in. He tried to convince me that I'd be better off at the condo—when we both know I'm the *last* person Carolyn would want around as a chaperon.'

'I'm sorry—' Regan's awkwardly expressed compassion caused a muscle to jump in his jaw, making him look markedly like his brother did when he was in a smouldering temper.

'Oh, so you're already in on that sordid family secret, are you?' he guessed bitterly. 'Josh is usually more discreet about his problems. I wouldn't have thought he was the type to indulge in careless pillow talk, but then neither did I think he regarded sex as a combat sport—'

'That's enough, Chris,' Joshua's voice crackled out as he came down the stairs two at a time, jumping the final distance and coming up behind Regan. 'There's no need to embarrass yourself more than you have already.'

'*I'm* not embarrassed.'

'Well, you should be. You're insulting a guest and I thought I'd taught you better manners. Come on, Regan, I'll give you a lift back to the house.'

'Why hustle her off in such a rush just because I've inconveniently turned up? Could it be *you're* the one embarrassed at being caught with your pants down?'

Joshua stepped in front of Regan, shielding her from his brother's crudity.

'You're asking for a punch in the mouth!'

'Why? Because I've found out the truth?' Chris said rawly. 'That you're not as lily-white as you like everyone to believe? I always knew you were a manipulative bastard, but to con Sir Frank into bringing your mistress up here so that you can flaunt your affair under Carolyn's unsuspecting nose—'

'I am not *flaunting* her, and she is *not* my mistress!'

'You're going to tell me you two were innocently playing checkers before I came on board? Don't make me laugh! Regan has your brand stamped all over her—God, she even *smells* of you.'

Regan went hot all over. She hoped he was talking about the expensive cologne!

'Dammit, Chris—'

'No—damn *you*! Don't you know how humiliated Caro would be if she knew? She *trusts* you, dammit!' His voice was thick with torment. 'She was so very quick to believe that *I* would let her down that she wouldn't listen to anything I said afterwards—but big Josh—oh, no, never! She really believes that *you're* the saint and *I'm* the sinner. And she *likes* Regan, she thinks of her as a friend…and all this time her new *friend* and her so-called fiancé have been—'

'*Don't* say it!' Joshua ground out as Chris teetered on the brink of obscenity.

His brother laughed harshly. 'I knew you were attracted to her, but I naively thought that—being such a stickler for men *doing the right thing* by their women—you'd merely suffer the tortures of the damned denying yourself.'

Instead of trying to douse the inflammatory situation with his cool reason, Joshua inexplicably chose to pour gasoline on the flames. 'Or, if I gave in to the attraction, that I'd feel compelled to confess all to Carolyn? Is that what you were *hoping* would happen, Chris? So that *you* could rush in and replay the big dramatic scene that you flubbed a couple of months ago, this time with *you* as the valiant saviour and me as the faithless villain? Forget it. You had your chance and blew it. As it happens, I've decided that Carolyn will make an ideal wife. There's a distinct commercial advantage in a businessman being associated with a beautiful, well-bred wife bouncing the evidence of his potent virility on her pretty knee...'

Regan felt Joshua's callous, careless taunt like a blow to her heart, but Chris looked utterly shattered. His young face was haggard as he looked at the brother he had idolised for so many years with an expression of pure loathing.

'You bastard. You think you're going to have it all, don't you? I won't let you do it! If you hurt Caro—'

'If you keep your mouth shut and mind your own business, she need never find out!' Joshua snapped. 'Get real, Chris—Carolyn may have been the embodiment of your boyish sexual fantasies, but, frankly, my tastes are a lot more mature. Now, if you don't mind, Regan and I will skip the rest of the moral lecture!'

Joshua was tight-lipped and broodingly morose on the way back to the house, and Regan made a coward of herself by pretending that she had a headache and ducking dinner. She had no wish to sit across the table from Carolyn and listen to her talk about her latest wedding dress fitting, or speculate feverishly on where Joshua might take her on their honeymoon.

But there was no avoiding the other woman early the next morning when she crashed into Regan's room just as she was finally managing to doze off after tossing and turning sleeplessly all night.

'What's the matter?' Regan asked blearily, struggling to sit up as Carolyn threw herself dramatically into the chair by the bed.

'I'm bleeding,' she moaned, and Regan's eyes snapped

wide, noticing the tear-tracks on Carolyn's normally flawless cheeks and her unnaturally pasty expression.

'My God, do you think you're having a miscarriage?'
she said, leaping out of bed.

'No—I'm *bleeding*—I've got my *period.*' Carolyn wrung
her slender hands and rocked to and fro in the chair. 'Oh,
God, Regan—what am I going to *do*?'

'But—but—you're *pregnant*...' Regan squawked, and
Carolyn shook her head.

'No—no, I'm not. It was a mistake—'

Regan collapsed on the side of the bed. 'A *mistake*? But
you had a test...'

'It was wrong. It happens—not often, the doctor says,
but it happens. I never went back for a physical examination, you see. But I started feeling some cramps yesterday
afternoon, and so I drove over to Granny's GP and...' her
big golden-brown eyes filled with tears '...and she said she
couldn't feel anything when she palpated me, so she sent
me for another test and it came back negative...'

Regan's brain was reeling. 'But, how could that
be...surely you had all the *symptoms*?'

'The doctor said sometimes a woman's body can mimic
the early physical signs if she really believes that she's
pregnant, and I did believe it—I did!' Carolyn's light con-
tralto rose sharply, as if to convince herself of her own
sincerity. 'My period didn't come and then I felt nauseous
nearly all the time, and my breasts started to feel sore and
I put on weight...of *course* I thought I was pregnant!' she
shrilled.

'The doctor said part of it was probably only fluid reten-
tion because my cycle was disturbed. I couldn't believe it—
I didn't dare tell anyone in case it turned out to be another
ghastly mistake. And then, when I woke up this morning...I
found I had my period! There is no baby—there never
was!' Her exultation held more than a hint of hysteria, and

a volatile mixture of joy, misery, relief and despair. 'I need never have had that fight with Chris. Oh, God, he's never going to want me *now*. He'll hate me even more than he does already. I put us all through this torture for *nothing*!' She buried her head in her hands, her hair falling around her body like a golden veil. Then she wrenched her tragic face up again. 'And Granny—the wedding! Regan—please help me…what do you think I should *do*?'

Regan forced herself to be calm, not to choke on the throttling hope that threatened to close off her air supply. 'The first thing you have to do,' she said carefully, 'is tell Joshua.'

Carolyn looked white-eyed with panic. 'Oh, no, I can't tell Jay!'

'Why can't you?' asked Regan hollowly. Was Carolyn now going to proclaim she'd fallen out of love with Chris and in love with Joshua?

'I just can't,' she babbled, clutching the arms of the chair. 'Not after all he's done for me. He and Chris had never had a serious argument in their lives until I came along, and now, because Jay stood up for me and tried to help me, even knowing how much I love Chris— Oh, God, neither of them are going to forgive me…it's all going to be so *humiliating*…you just don't *understand*!'

Better a little humiliation now than a lifetime of unhappiness ahead, thought Regan acidly. How in the world had Carolyn thought she could be happy in a marriage that would have made her a sister to the man she still truly loved? How could even Joshua have been so arrogant as to believe he could *make* Carolyn content with such a situation? It was a recipe for emotional disaster whether or not the estrangement between the brothers remained permanent.

'No, I don't understand,' she said steadily. 'But I *do* know that you can't go through with the wedding with Joshua still thinking that you're going to have his brother's baby. You must know how he feels about honesty. Remember what happened last time he married a woman who tried to use a pregnancy to manipulate him? As a matter of honour—his *and* yours—you *have* to tell him.'

'He'll think I'm a moron—so will Chris!'

'Chris is a doctor, for goodness' sake—he should have considered the possibility of something like this and insisted you both reserve any decisions until you'd had a proper examination. Of course, that would have been the *rational* thing to do, and people in love aren't always rational.'

Carolyn's eyes suddenly went dreamy. 'No...that's true... I know I sprung it on him badly, when we were in the middle of a fight about something else, and he felt cornered—but so did I! Maybe I should tell *Chris* first. After all, it was supposed to be his baby—and *he* could tell Jay...'

Regan eyed her cynically. 'I don't think it's the sort of thing Joshua would appreciate hearing second-hand.'

All Regan's advice seemed to fall on deaf ears, and by the time she went downstairs she had a real headache, which suddenly got worse when Sir Frank greeted her in the breakfast room with cheerful congratulations on her excellent timing—because Joshua had just arrived and was waiting to see her in the library.

'I put him in there because he said it was business and he wanted somewhere you wouldn't be disturbed. I hope he's not going to try and poach you away from Harriman's before the takeover—but then, that would sort of be like poaching you away from himself, wouldn't it?'

His chuckle followed her down the hall, but Regan didn't feel at all like laughing. As soon as she walked into the library and saw Ryan standing slouched beside the desk, nervously pushing his glasses up his nose, her heart sank.

Joshua, standing behind the desk, threw a sheaf of computer printouts on the desk, scattering them like confetti.

'Perhaps you'd like to explain these?' Icicles dripped from every syllable.

Out of the corner of her eye Regan could see Ryan wince. Whatever he had done, against her express instructions, she knew she couldn't let him take any of the blame. 'I—what are they?'

Joshua's fist crashed down on top of the papers, the ice melting to reveal the molten volcano of temper beneath.

'Don't compound your lies by pretending innocence!' he roared. 'No *wonder* you were so eager to join me on the boat yesterday. It provided you with the perfect alibi!' He raked her with a look of searing contempt. 'You had my son back at the office doing your dirty work for you, while you kept me safely out of the way. I compliment you on your technique—suborn the son and seduce the father.'

Regan had done neither, but she could see he was in no mood to listen. She tentatively picked up one of the pieces of paper. 'But, surely, you must be able to see—'

He lunged forward and dashed it from her hands. 'I *see*, all right!' he erupted. 'I see that you *used* him...you used *my son*—' in his ungovernable outrage, his passionate protectiveness towards his family had never been more apparent '—to cover up a crime! You used his feelings for you to make him an accessory to fraud. When I found these in his room this morning I knew that *I* was the fool being taken for a ride yesterday.'

'But, Dad, I told you—Regan said she didn't want me to—'

'Be quiet, son, you're in deep enough trouble as it is! What Regan *says* and what she *means* are two different things.' He swung his attention back to her guilty white face. 'Was this a set-up right from the beginning—from that first night in my apartment?'

Regan rallied, as outraged as he by the notion. '*No!* You know it *couldn't* have been!'

'And you expect me to believe you?' he slashed sardonically, but seemed to accept that his accusation was incompatible with subsequent events as he went on, 'Serendipity, then, when you were given the chance to come to Palm Cove and realised that you might use our former...*liaison* to help create a smokescreen for your actions. Were those sexual tricks you performed on me yesterday supposed to be your version of a personal insurance policy? Designed to make me reluctant to summon the police in the event of your being found out—'

'*Joshua!*' she gasped in agonised protest, glancing meaningfully at Ryan, who was following the conversation back and forth with a deep, and noticeably unrepentant fascination.

Her concern seemed only to trigger an even greater fury. 'What? Do you think we might be corrupting his innocence? It's a little late to worry about that, isn't it? I think, for his own future protection, it's about time he learned the difference between an honest woman and a conniving little whore!'

CHAPTER TEN

'LEAVE? But you don't have to *leave*!'

Sir Frank's bluff response to her miserable confession made Regan feel marginally better. Her coruscating encounter with Joshua had ended shortly after his ugly outburst, when he had seemed to recognise that his inability to control his rising fury at her brave defence of her character rendered him unacceptably vulnerable in his son's eyes—and his own. He had stormed out of the house leaving a dozen menacing threats hanging in the air, with a stunned Ryan mouthing silent apologies and flapping cryptic hand-signals to Regan that she presumed were meant to be reassuring as he was frog-marched to the door.

It had all happened so fast that Regan had felt as if she had been the victim of a lightning razor attack—there had been no pain, only a numb shock as she'd contemplated her numerous slicing wounds. She had limped back to the dining room and summoned the presence of mind to make a clean breast about Michael's theft, and her failed efforts to replace the money, to an astonished Sir Frank and Hazel.

She hadn't mentioned Ryan, merely saying that Joshua had discovered what she was doing, and she had been staggered when, instead of accusing her of aiding and abetting her husband's crime, or condemning her stupidity, the Harrimans had rallied round with shocked support.

At her implacable insistence, Sir Frank had reluctantly accepted her resignation, but he was baulking at her proposal to immediately return to Auckland.

'Of course I do,' she said proudly. 'You trusted me and I've let you down.'

'Not you—that wretched bounder Michael!' Sir Frank growled in his quaintly old-fashioned terminology. 'If it's a matter of the money, don't you worry about it, lass. You know I'll see things right.'

She clung to the wreckage of her pride, devastated by the unexpected expression of faith. 'No...I have the bank cheque for the full repayment upstairs; I'll give it to you before I leave—'

'Now, Regan, you know we won't turn away from you just because you made a wrong choice under stress,' said Hazel gently. 'It's your intentions that count, and we understand that you were just trying to do what you thought was best. You've paid much too dearly for Michael's sins as it is, so you don't have to go on covering yourself in shame...'

Regan swallowed hard, overwhelmed by her kindness. She had thought that the Harrimans would be glad to see the back of her. And no doubt they would if they knew the true extent of her shame! As for the wedding—Regan didn't know what was going to happen on that score and was desperate not to care.

'I'm sorry...but I know Joshua won't agree with you. I realise I'm letting you down double-fold, but—'

'But nothing!' said Sir Frank. 'I'm sure Wade will come round once he cools down and hears all the mitigating factors.'

'He knows them already,' said Regan tightly, afraid she was going to burst into tears.

'Well, you've admitted everything and done everything in your power to put things right—that puts you on the side of the angels as far as I'm concerned, and I'll tell him so,' he gruffed.

'It's not just that.' She knew she was going to have to come up with a definitive argument. 'I'm afraid I've also fallen in love with Joshua,' she said flatly. 'It's very awkward and embarrassing, and I'm sorry to complicate matters, but I really think it would be better all round if I went home...'

Her honesty paid off. Sir Frank continued to bluster in a muted kind of way, but Hazel instantly empathised with the horror of an unrequited love. She hugged Regan, delivering a blizzard of sympathetic assurances that *of course* she understood her urgent desire to leave, and of course she could manage without her, especially now that she had discarded her crutch and was hobbling about on her rapidly improving ankle.

Regan packed and was gone within the hour, driven back to Auckland by Alice Beatson's lanky, monosyllabic husband Steve.

Fortunately, Lisa and Saleena were at work when he dropped her off at the flat, for, once inside, her fragile façade of dignity shattered and Regan indulged herself in a storm of weeping, the bitter culmination of months of pain and strain to which had now been added this wrenching new loss, greater than all the others added together.

When the fit of anguish was over her throat was raw, her face looked like soggy puff pastry and her bones ached as if she had been beaten all over with a baseball bat. Her throat was soothed with lemon and honey, and her face marginally improved with a cool wash, but she knew the ache wasn't really physical. Until the psychological bruising came out she knew she wouldn't feel much better, however much she cried, and there was no way that she knew to hurry the healing.

If she could have despised Joshua it would have been so much easier, but she understood him far too well. From his perspective he was perfectly justified in questioning her morals and suspecting her motives, and the fact that her actions had placed his son in jeopardy would be impossible for him to forgive. As he had once told her so forcefully, no one got a second chance to breach his trust.

The odds had been impossibly stacked against her from the very beginning. She had known that loving him was a one-way ticket to heartbreak...but, oh, the joy that she had experienced along the way was almost worth the price of arrival!

The next few days were spent compulsively trying not to think about anything or anyone connected with Palm Cove, which was next to impossible when she half expected a policeman to come knocking at the door...or for Joshua to come bursting in, a one-man posse on a quest for the modern version of frontier justice. He hadn't exactly ordered her not to leave town, but that had been the gist of his final threat as he had left the house. And when she had arrived home she had been horrified to realise that she was still wearing his expensive platinum watch—another crime for him to lay at her door! And this time he would be right, for she had deliberately done nothing about returning it. By now Sir Frank would have arranged for her cheque to be repaid into the company accounts, but she was afraid to hope that that would be the end of it, not if Joshua felt it incumbent on his honour to exact personal retribution.

Desperate to avoid having to deal with reality, she impressed on Lisa and Saleena she wasn't in to phone calls—from *anyone*—and whenever they went out she switched off the answer-machine and took the phone off the hook. She did, however, make one stilted call to Cindy, to tell her that the money had been repaid, and that whatever repercussions there might be from now on would stop with Regan. She had hung up on Cindy's hysterical thanks in the certain knowledge that she had finally closed the book on her failed marriage.

The following afternoon, on the fourth day of her emo-

tional exile, her brittle shell was cracked by the last person
she would have expected to bother to seek her out—Carolyn Harriman, floating on air after her final wedding gown
fitting.

'Hi—you don't mind I got your address from Granny,
do you?' she chirped to Regan, who *did* mind. She had
refused to wonder if Carolyn had yet plucked up the courage to break the news of her phantom pregnancy, guiltily
aware that she had fled without even saying goodbye—
unwilling to risk any additional emotional trauma.

'I couldn't get through on the phone, but I figured you
wouldn't have another job yet and thought you could probably do with some cheering up,' breezed Carolyn. 'Look—
I bought Danish pastries to go with our afternoon coffee!
Granny told me why you left—about the rotten thing your
husband did to you. God, men can be utter pigs, can't
they?'

Regan could detect no hint of falsity in her friendly attitude, and was forced to conclude that Chris must not have
blabbed about what he had seen on board the *Sara Wade*.

It struck her that she had never seen the young woman
looking more relaxed as she leant on the stove while Regan
put the jug on to boil.

'You're still going ahead with it, then?' she said warily,
when she learned where Carolyn had been.

Only Carolyn could simper without looking silly. 'Well,
yes—sort of… Haven't you got a percolator?'

'No, we haven't. What do you mean, *sort* of?' Regan
forced herself to ask.

'Uh…with a different groom.'

Regan's teaspoonful of instant coffee spilled all over the
bench.

'*Chris?*'

'*Of course* Chris.' Carolyn sounded ludicrously offended
that she should ask. At Regan's expression she offered up

a sheepish smile and waggled the new ruby and diamond ring on her finger, 'Luckily he kept this when I threw it back in his face. We got re-engaged a couple of days ago.'

'And J-Joshua raised no objections?' Regan stuttered.

'Why should he?' said Carolyn smugly. 'It's what he expected all along. Why do you think he bribed the printer to muck up the invitations? He told me when he proposed that he doubted we'd have to actually marry each other. He said he knew that when it came to the crunch Chris loved me too much to let me marry anyone else!'

'How omniscient of him,' said Regan, shards of anger thrusting jaggedly up through a smothering blanket of pain. And he had had the nerve to rage at *her* for being conniving! She hadn't been the only one with a secret agenda!

'Well, he was *right*, wasn't he?' Carolyn defended. 'And if he *had* been wrong, then he *was* prepared to genuinely go through with it, for the baby's sake—and for that I'll always be grateful to him! It was really strange, though, because he's been in a really *filthy* mood about everything else in last few days, but he hardly reacted at all when I fronted up about not being pregnant. He acted like it wasn't even *important*. He just shrugged and suggested I tell Chris as soon as possible, so I did, and instead of rowing about it we talked and talked for hours, and admitted that we had both behaved immaturely and I cried and...' she almost managed a blush '...we ended up in bed.

'Oh, Regan, you should have heard what he said! He said that he'd been miserable without me and mad with jealousy when I turned to Jay, that's why he'd been so nasty! He said that he'd been forced to face up to the fact he hadn't been fair to me *or* to Jay. He said he'd have kidnapped me at the altar rather than let Jay have me!'

The idea of Joshua being humiliated in front of two hundred guests had a certain vicious appeal, thought Regan, even if it would have been partly at his own instigation!

She stuffed herself with fattening pastries as she masochistically encouraged Carolyn to happily twitter on, gleaning the fact that Joshua and Ryan were still staying at Palm Cove and that Hazel had conscripted a biddable niece of Alice's to be her letter-writer. Carolyn herself had made the trip down to her Auckland couturier in the WadeCo helicopter, and she gave Regan a nervous rash when she let slip that she had shared it with Joshua, who was expecting to stay overnight in the city and resume permanent residence in a matter of days.

As she departed, basking in her own happiness, Carolyn gave Regan a hand-addressed silver-gilt wedding invitation.

'Chris says you have to come,' she told her gaily. 'He told me to deliver it to you personally and tell you that he'll have something to say if you try to refuse!'

Regan gave her a sharp look, but Carolyn seemed to be unaware of any ulterior meaning to her words. The Wade brothers seemed to have a pretty similar line in ambiguous threats, thought Regan savagely as she closed the door and immediately picked up the telephone receiver and slammed it back on the hook. No more avoiding life!

It immediately began to ring, and she snatched it up with a belligerent snarl.

A startled silence. 'Hello…uh…is that Regan?'

She sucked in a wild breath. 'Yes, who is this?'

'Derek… You know—Derek Clarke.'

'Oh.' Her heart flip-flopped in her chest. 'Do you want Cleo? She's not here—'

'No, actually, I wanted to talk to you. A really weird thing just happened to me…'

Regan felt like snapping that a lot of weird things probably happened to sleaze-bags like himself.

'Oh, what was that?' she asked with immense restraint.

'Well…it's this guy I sometimes arrange dates for—he

just sent me an e-mail to say he wants me to set him up with someone called Eve tonight…'

The furious roaring in Regan's ears made it difficult to hear him as he went on, 'So of course I immediately zapped him with the fact that I don't *know* any women called Eve and—this is the weird part—he comes back on my instant message system with *your* name. I told him that he had to be mistaken, because I knew you weren't much of a swinger, but he wasn't interested in anyone else. He was real insistent that it had to be *you* and only you. He said all he wanted me to do was give you the message that Adam needs to meet you at the same time and place. No other name or specifics—just Adam—and he said, to quote him exactly here: ''Tell Eve she can name her own terms.'' So I thought, what the hell! I've got nothing to lose by *asking*—'

'I'll do it!'

'After all, you can't very well slap my face over the— *What did you say?*'

Regan firmed up her quavering voice. 'I said, I'll do it. E-mail him back and tell *Adam* that he's got a deal!'

The marble foyer on the fourteenth floor was as coldly stark as Regan remembered it, and the deep-set door just as intimidating, but this time when she rang the bell Regan didn't hesitate.

She might be crazy to take this chance, but she would be insane not to! Joshua had approached her through a neutral intermediary in a way that gave her the option of accepting or refusing to meet him. In the circumstances, she supposed that using Derek might be considered an implicit threat, but Regan didn't see it that way. She viewed the offer through the optimistic eyes of love. Trying to duplicate the exact conditions of their first meeting might be Joshua's oblique way of saying that he wanted them to start afresh, to rewrite their history together. It would be typical of that sophisticated, ironic sense of humour, tinged with unexpected mischief, with which she had fallen in love!

He had said Adam *needed* to see Eve, and that she could name her own terms—that didn't sound like someone aggressively seeking revenge. It sounded alluringly close to begging. Perhaps, for once in his life, Joshua was willing to entrust someone with a second chance...

She might be walking into a trap, but if there was *any* prospect, however small, of *any* kind of future relationship with the man she loved, Regan owed it to herself to find out.

As she waited for the doorbell to be answered she didn't allow herself any romantic fantasies. Now that he was an unencumbered bachelor again, it was highly likely that Joshua might just be on the prowl for some no-holds-barred, guilt-free sex from an occasional mistress...

Well, she hadn't found much security as a wife, thought Regan defiantly, maybe she'd be better off as a rich man's mistress!

She had her smile all ready for the man who opened the door.

'Hello, Pierre.'

'Mam'selle Regan!' His turtle-mouth gaped open and shut.

'Actually, it's Eve,' she teased. 'Do I have to produce a card this time—or are you just going to invite me in?'

'Mam'selle!' His voice crackled with reproach and she laughed, a soft, clear, lilting sound, tinged with excitement, that stole into the apartment ahead of her. Instead of responding, Pierre looked back over his shoulder, and Regan, impatient with the delay, took the opportunity to slip under his arm and stroll inside.

'Uh, *mam'selle*, you must wait to be announced—' Pierre let go of the door and darted across her path.

She laughed again. 'Oh, you mean you're not going to tell me he's delayed in some business meeting somewhere and ply me your fantastic canapés while I wait?'

He frowned. 'Really, Mam'selle R—Eve—I think you should let me—'

He was interrupted by a deep voice floating up around the glass-brick stairwell.

'Who is it, Pierre?

Joshua came springing casually up the steps in shirt-sleeves and the grey trousers of a suit, glancing over what looked like an architectural plan in his hand. When he looked up from what he was reading and caught sight of Regan he froze in mid-step. His face was unguarded for a split second during which Regan saw a shock of incredulity tauten the skin across the bones of his skull.

'Regan?'

She looked from his wary face to Pierre's uncharacteristically deadpan expression and it hit her, then, with humiliating force: both men were so stunned to see her that it was evident her arrival was totally unexpected.

That e-mail *hadn't* been an invitation, *or* a trap—because Joshua had obviously never sent it! And Regan had been so eager to believe that he wanted to see her again that she had never entertained the idea that it might have a cruel joke perpetrated by someone else entirely!

Oh, *God*!

Her confidence smashed into a million tiny pieces as Joshua's gaze dipped, his eyes suddenly narrowing with predatory sharpness as he recognised the combination of classic black sheath, black stockings and gold-heeled evening sandals. Even the bag she was carrying was the same one she had been carrying *That Night*.

'Regan?' This time his voice was redolent with heated speculation, and a hint of amusement.

A hot flood of embarrassment welled up in her soul as

she sought to extricate herself from her gross folly. She couldn't bear to be the object of his derision. 'I—I'm sorry, I—this is a mistake.'

Joshua was up the rest of steps in a flash, the sheet of paper he had been holding wafting unnoticed to the floor. 'What makes you say that?'

She tried to back away and stepped on Pierre's foot, ignoring his yelp. 'I—I must have come to the wrong door...' she invented absurdly.

Joshua looked at her provocative garb. 'Did you want the elderly grandmother to the left of me, or the gay art director on the right?' he asked gravely.

'Floor. I said the wrong *floor*,' she quickly corrected herself, putting her hand to her throat to cover the fluttering pulse on which he seemed to be fixated.

Another mistake. He saw the watch—*his* watch—still strapped to her wrist and smiled, as if he knew that she hadn't taken it off for even a second since the day he had given it—*lent* it—to her...as if he knew that she lay in bed each night with her hand tucked under her cheek, the almost inaudible ticking a lullaby that sang her into her dreams of the man to whom it—and she—belonged.

'Well, why don't we make the most of your Freudian slip?' he purred. 'Won't you come in and have a drink for old times' sake?'

She frantically shook her head, and he lowered his voice to a coaxing murmur.

'Please...' He held out a hand, palm up. 'Eve...one drink with me?'

Unable to trust herself to speak, Regan continued to shake her head, resisting the explicit invitation in his eyes and voice.

'To keep me company...' he appealed, and thrust his outstretched hand into his trouser pocket and produced a set of keys. 'Because Pierre was just going out—weren't you, Pierre?'

He tossed the keys through the air and Pierre fielded them in one hand. 'To be sure, *m'sieur.*'

'Have a good time, and don't forget to set the deadlock when you leave—I don't want anyone breaking in on me while you're gone…'

Pierre had already slipped out of the door before Regan realised the implications of the message that had been passed over her head. She grabbed at the heavy brass handle but it was too late; the door refused to even rattle on its hinge.

She closed her anguished eyes, raising her fist to rest it helplessly against the wood.

'You must see that now that you're here I can't let you go,' he said quietly.

'No, I don't see!' she cried. 'I told you, my being here is a mistake—'

'Dressed like that? I don't think so,' he said with that same awful, quiet certainty. 'You came here to see me, didn't you? And you came in the persona of Eve, because Eve isn't as vulnerable as Regan.'

She whirled around, her back flat against the barrier to her freedom. 'What do you know?' she scorned proudly.

But his eyes weren't gloating or triumphant, they were beautifully solemn. 'About you? Not enough, it seems. About me? Not as much as I thought I did. I thought I had everything under control, including myself. I was wrong. Quite spectacularly wrong.'

He approached her soft-footed, holding her captive with that hypnotic gaze. 'By the way, you might be interested to learn that I'm not marrying Carolyn.'

'I know, I saw her this morning—' She broke off, biting her lip as she saw his eyes light up at the nugget of information. Now he was *really* locking himself into the mind-set that she had come rushing over here to grovel for his attention.

'I'm a cynical swine,' he continued, on his original course. 'Experience has taught me that it's safer to expect the worst of people instead of trusting to the best—'

'Is this an apology?' Regan cut him off stonily. All she could think was: *He didn't invite you here.* He thought *she* had come crawling back to *him.*

He met her aggression with a soft answer. 'Oh, I think you'll find it's much more than that. Won't you come in and sit down? You may as well accept that I have no intention of unlocking that door—even if I did know where Pierre kept his keys.'

He held out his hand again, but she ignored it as she stalked past him down the stairs. He allowed her to evade him until they reached the level of the sunken lounge, then his fingers curled around her elbow as he turned her to face him.

She tried to jerk it away. 'Don't touch me!'

'I can't help it,' he said, cupping her other elbow and drawing her towards him. 'It's a compulsion. Since the first time I met you I can't be near you without wanting to have my hands on you. You churn me up, and in the beginning I wasn't sure I liked that; I wasn't prepared for it—it interfered with my plans. I wanted to be able to push what I felt for you aside until I was ready to deal with it. But do you know what I've found that I don't like even *more*, Regan…?'

What I feel for you? She shook her head, dazed with feverish apprehension, her eyes huge in her face, unable to believe that this was real and not just a figment of her reckless imagination.

'I don't like you being away from me. I don't like not having you around to churn me up—to intrigue me, infuriate me, comfort me, excite me and, yes—to enrage me.

Even when I'm furious with you I still want you near me...'

She began to tremble and he eased himself into contact, his trousers brushing her legs. 'I don't like knowing that I hurt you. That I prated on about family responsibility and honour and then failed to respect that you felt a duty to protect *yours*. I'm so used to people expecting *me* to handle their problems for them that I didn't know how to act when I ran up against someone who was so determined *not* to demand anything of me. I should have admired you for having the courage of your convictions and for your stubborn loyalty. Instead I was furious that you'd continued to squander it on that crooked bastard you married rather than transferring it to *me*, even though I'd done nothing to earn it! I knew I couldn't afford to make another mistake with you, so I've spent the last few days racking my brains to think of a logical reason I might use to persuade you to see me again.'

His fingers tightened and his voice roughened. 'But it isn't logic you want from me, is it, Regan? You can't imagine how I felt when I saw you just now, when I realised that you'd been willing to sacrifice your pride to reach out to me, even after the contemptible way I treated you, that your desire to be with me was so strong that it conquered all your fears—'

'Don't!' she choked, her fierce elation tempered by the knowledge she was a fraud.

His tender smile was a kiss upon her sight. 'You're going to stop me now? When I'm humbling myself for you?'

'It's not necessary—'

'But it is. For me, it is. You've done your bit, now it's my turn to do the risking.'

Much as she longed to let him do just that, she had to put him right before he went any further! 'Joshua—'

She turned her head, searching for the right words, and

suddenly caught sight of the frozen picture on the big-screen television behind him. 'What's that?'

Joshua let her go and quickly scooped up the video remote control from the arm of a chair, pointing it at the machine.

'Wait a minute.' Regan snatched it out of his hand as she looked at the freeze-frame. 'That's *me*!'

She moved around for a better look and swallowed a fuzzy feeling in her throat as she pressed the 'pause' button and her screen self began to move. 'That's the security video from the night I was here!' she whispered as she watched herself tentatively step out of the apartment building lift.

Joshua sighed. 'It's the only picture I have of you,' he said simply, and her eyes stung as he turned his brooding gaze back at the screen. 'You look a little nervous here, don't you?' he murmured. 'I've watched it over and over, and I definitely think the lady is having some second thoughts, but look there—see—she squares her shoulders and decides: What the hell! I'm going to go for it...'

He was watching the screen, but Regan was watching his softened face. She imagined him sitting here all alone, surrounded by every luxury money could buy, replaying those same few seconds of videotape over and over again, studying her every move and trying to analyse her thoughts, and her heart surrendered itself for ever into his keeping.

'Oh, *Josh*...' She wrapped her arms around him, wanting to protect him from ever being lonely again. Whatever he felt for her, she loved him enough for the both of them.

'Now you know how I recognised Ryan had a crush on you,' he said wryly, tipping her face up to meet his. 'I felt the same way—only mine was the fully-fledged adult version. After that first night I was going to find out who you really were, and make arrangements to see you again,' he confessed. 'But then Carolyn called and events overtook me. But you still haunted the back of my mind. So much so that I thought I was hallucinating when I first saw you out the window at Hazel's.'

She told him about Ryan and the tree, and he laughed. 'No wonder he took to you so quickly. Hide-and-go-seek used to be one of his favourite games.

'And speaking of favourite games...' He leaned forward and whispered teasingly into her ear, 'Are you wearing anything under that dress?'

Regan went utterly scarlet and he stilled, his eyes widening with stunned admiration as he realised the daring wickedness with which she had hoped to seduce him.

'You're *not*?' he guessed, erupting into more, very sexy laughter as she shook her head and hid her scalding face in the front of his silk shirt. His hand slid down to trace her shapely naked bottom through the dress. 'My God, you did come prepared for battle, didn't you, honey? I never stood a chance!'

She remembered what it was so important for her to make clear and lifted her hot face. 'It wasn't actually my idea to come here tonight,' she told him, her eyes daring him to take back anything he had said. She told him about Derek's call regarding the e-mail. 'Naturally, I thought it'd come from *you*,' she said, thinking that a sleaze-bag made a rather unlikely cupid. 'I thought *you* were making the first move.'

Joshua's response was a slight touch of colour on his hard cheekbones, but he was too smug at the serendipitous outcome and too intrigued by the puzzle to be truly embarrassed by his error—the supremely arrogant assumption that had prompted him to reveal his deepest emotions.

'If he was responding to my private Internet address then he would have presumed so, too. I don't know what's on there at the moment because I don't check my personal messages every day. Ryan's always on my back about—'

He broke off and backed out of her arms. 'Excuse me a minute!' He was a lot longer than a minute, but when he had finally hung up the phone and came back to her after his low-voiced conversation his eyes were glowing with dangerous amusement.

'My son's doing. It seems that Ryan suffers from a God complex.' His ruefulness was an irresistible temptation.

'I can't imagine where he got that from!' murmured Regan

He quelled her with the lift of an eyebrow. 'Apparently he cracked the password on my e-mail account some time back and decided to use it to set us up.'

'But—how could he know about—? Or that we called each other Adam and Eve?' she gulped.

He ran a hand through his hair and slanted her a look that was charmingly abashed. 'I had drink or three too many that night I lost my temper…after I found out you'd skipped out on me *again*,' he confessed. 'I got a little rowdy—and drunkenly maudlin, according to Ryan—in my lecture to him on the evils of doe-eyed women who lead men around by the uh—certain parts of their male anatomy. He says I mentioned that Derek Clarke had arranged for us to meet…and I also mentioned that we had jokingly appropriated our middle names…'

'You mentioned an awful lot to an impressionable fifteen-year-old-boy,' Regan said ominously.

'Yes, well…' Joshua shed his chagrin in a little spurt of paternal pride. 'I suppose his super-intelligence filled in most of the gaps and the rest just took a little research—for example, your full name is bound to be on the database at Harriman Developments, and as *you* well know my son doesn't see privacy laws as a barrier to his investigations. Give him a computer, a modem and enough time, and Ryan could well rule the world.'

'But *why*?' Regan said, not wanting to think that Ryan

had *intended* for her to be hurt and humiliated by his father. 'He *knew* that we parted on terrible terms.'

Joshua sighed. 'That was why. He thought it was his fault, and that, with Carolyn out of the picture, if he could just get us together, propinquity would do the rest—although he had a rather more basic term for it...'

Regan put her hands over her still warm cheeks. 'He must think I'm an awful tramp.'

He took pity on her mortification and took her back in his arms to kiss the tip of her pink nose. 'I think he thinks you're a very sexy woman whom his father is crazy about. He said to tell you, by the way, that he never broke his promise to you—what he did was *not* "dumb and misguided"—it was extremely clever; it was keeping the hard copy evidence that did him in!'

'Still, what if you hadn't wanted to see me?' she worried.

His voice was warm with disbelief. 'Darling, the boy watched me skewer you with a knife and then listened to me prose on about you for hours while I ploughed my way through half a bottle of Scotch. I assure you, he was in no doubt as to what I was going to do when I got my hands on you again.'

'Throttle me?'

His hands tightened around her waist as his mouth came down on hers. 'Never let you go.'

'Oh...' Bliss was a warm mouth and a strong pair of arms.

'So, does that mean you're willing to accept my son?' he murmured against her throat.

'I've already accepted he's your son,' she replied, confused.

'No, I mean...as your own. I think all the children of one family should call the same person Mother.' He lifted his head as she stiffened in his encircling arms. 'Did you think I wasn't going to ask the woman I love to marry me?

Especially one as elusive as you—what kind of idiot do you take me for?'

Her small face was incandescent with joy. 'I think you're a pure genius. I guess that's why I love you.'

It was the first time she had said it out loud, but instead of the expected romantic response, Joshua raised a challenging eyebrow. 'Prove it.'

She laughed, and kicked off her shoes, and raced him into the bedroom. As she wrestled him playfully onto the bed he murmured, 'The last time I entertained Eve in here, she was too proud to accept anything from me. I hope this time will be different.'

'"Pride comes before a fall,"' quoted Regan.

He smiled. 'Don't I know it!' He traced her kiss-swollen mouth with a gentle finger. 'So…is your pride willing to be flexible for me tonight?'

'Have you still got that gorgeous tennis bracelet?' she teased.

His eyes glinted. 'You're not really allergic to gold, are you?' And when she shook her head he pulled out the bedside drawer and began dragging out boxes and shaking them open over her prone body—bracelets, necklaces, lockets, bangles, brooches falling in an extravagant rain over her black dress.

'Josh!' She sifted them through her fingers with a laughing protest.

'Not enough?' He produced more, until she was heaped with splendour and helpless with giggles.

'I bought them all because you don't have any jewellery and I wasn't sure what you'd like best,' he said with perfect seriousness. 'I want to give you everything, you see,' he said roughly. 'Me—life, love, babies galore…everything that it's in my power to give you.' Then he took out one last item, a folded piece of creased tissue paper, and carefully unwrapped it, and she sat up, shedding the expensive baubles, to look at the thin, old-gold band plainly set with a straight row of three extremely modest diamonds.

'It was my mother's engagement ring, and her mother's before her,' he said. 'Dad kept it for me after Mum died so I could give it in turn to my wife. But Clare thought it was too old-fashioned and the diamonds too small. And I never even considered showing it to Carolyn. For the last fifteen years, although I didn't know it, I've been keeping it for you...'

'It's beautiful,' said Regan shakily, imagining all the emotion invested in the cherished reminder of loves past.

He slid it on her slender finger. 'I knew it would suit you...'

'Small, plain and simple?' she taunted his ruthless pride.

'Dainty, rare and precious.' He tumbled her back on the bed and carelessly brushed away his lavish offerings in order to get down to the serious business of loving.

'Do you know, I think that you and I together have helped prove an old saying?' he said, lifting the hand bearing his ring to his lips.

'What's that?' she murmured dreamily as he bent his head to give her the most treasured gift of all.

'That revenge *is* deliciously, irresistibly sweet...'

HARLEQUIN PRESENTS®

EXPECTING!

She's sexy, she's successful... and she's pregnant!

Relax and enjoy these new stories about spirited women and gorgeous men, whose passion results in pregnancies... sometimes unexpectedly! All the new parents-to-be will discover that the business of making babies brings with it the most special love of all....

September 1999—**Having Leo's Child** #2050
by Emma Darcy

October 1999—**Having His Babies** #2057
by Lindsay Armstrong

November 1999—**The Boss's Baby** #2064
by Miranda Lee

December 1999—**The Yuletide Child** #2070
by Charlotte Lamb

Available wherever Harlequin books are sold.

HARLEQUIN®
Makes any time special ™

Coming Next Month

HARLEQUIN ◆ PRESENTS®

THE BEST HAS JUST GOTTEN BETTER!

#2067 A CONVENIENT BRIDEGROOM Helen Bianchin
(Society Weddings)
In her marriage of convenience to Carlo Santangelo, Aysha
knew she'd gain wealth, status and the sexiest husband ever!
Aysha loved her fiancé and wanted a real marriage, but would
Carlo give up his glamorous mistress...?

#2068 LOVER BY DECEPTION Penny Jordan
(Sweet Revenge/Seduction)
When Anna Trewayne lost her memory, she mistakenly
believed Ward Hunter to be a friend and lover. She'd
welcomed him into her arms...her bed...but what would
happen when her memory returned?

#2069 A MARRIAGE BETRAYED Emma Darcy
Kristy longed to find her natural family, but instead she found
Armand Dutournier, who wanted revenge for a betrayal she
hadn't committed. Did that mean she had a twin? Was he the
only lead to the family she yearned for?

#2070 THE YULETIDE CHILD Charlotte Lamb
(Expecting!)
Dylan had been thrilled when she'd married handsome
Ross Jefferson after a whirlwind romance. But she'd also
moved out of town and become unexpectedly pregnant.
Worse—her husband seemed to be having an affair....

#2071 MISTLETOE MISTRESS Helen Brooks
Joanne refused to have an affair with her sexy, arrogant
boss, Hawk Mallen. But then he offered her a dream
promotion—with one catch: she was at his command day
and night. Could she resist such a tempting proposal?

#2072 THE FAITHFUL WIFE Diana Hamilton
Jake and Bella, once happily married, have been separated a
whole year. Now Jake and Bella are tricked into spending
Christmas together. Isolated, they discover the passion is
still there—but can they overcome their past?